DAVNOK'S DISSENSION.

I0591082

ABOUT THE AUTHOR.

Grigory Fozimir is an adventure fiction writer and translator. He has also translated Jules Verne's *Master Zacharius, Gil Braltar, A Drama in the Air*.

GRIGORY FOZIMIR.

DAVNOK'S DISSENSION:

AN ESPIONAGE NOVELLA.

SECOND EDITION
WITH MINOR REVISIONS.

WITH AN ILLUSTRATION BY
H. TOUSSAINT.

INCLUDES A NEW AUTHOR'S ADVERTISEMENT.

TEPLEV BOOKS.
TEPLEV MEDIA PTY. LTD.
MELBOURNE.
2024.

Teplev Books.
Published by Teplev Media Pty. Ltd., Melbourne, Australia.
www.teplevmedia.com

First edition published by Teplev Media Pty. Ltd. 2018.
Second edition with minor revisions published 2024.
Copyright © Grigory Fozimir, 2018, 2024. All rights reserved.

Typeset in Libre Baskerville.

A catalog record for this book is available from the National Library of Australia.

I.S.B.N.: 978-0-6483379-4-2 (paperback)

I-01.12.2024

AUTHOR'S ADVERTISEMENT.

This little story is a hot potato of thrilling exploits and provocative ideas! Do you like a compelling protagonist, deadly foes, and conflicting motivations which quickly escalate and clash at cross-purposes? Do you like a quick pace, a tight narrative, and captivating characters confronted with monumental challenges? These exciting features all lie waiting, dear reader, within these pages!

What started out as an exercise in writing a realistic yet gripping spy fiction plot led me,—unexpectedly yet inexorably,—to discover the true legal power structure of the United Nations, and to learn how this reveals the organization's alleged purpose, "to maintain international peace and security," to be a totally meaningless platitude; nothing more than a hollow marketing buzz phrase! And who really controls the United Nations? My goodness! what a shock to my naive and propagandized soul all these terrible discoveries were! And what a terrific shock to Davnok when he also stumbles across these ugly truths on his treacherous quest!

But does Davnok draw accurate conclusions about the United Nations' true purpose? Does he make the right decisions in his attempt to rectify the situation and do some good in the world? Is he close to the mark with his political surmisals? These questions, the above discoveries, and the above features are my offerings, dear reader. This is an invitation to join Davnok on his journey to Strasbourg, to put yourself in his shoes, to face the same challenges he and his companions face, and to ask and think for yourself: "How can we make the world a more peaceful and prosperous place?"

Grigory Fozimir.

Melbourne, August 2024.

DEFINITIONAL NOTE.

espionage.

NOUN. 1. the systematic use of spies to obtain secret information, esp. by governments to discover military or political secrets.
Collins English Dictionary, sixth edition.

DAVNOK'S DISSENSION.

I.

MELBOURNE, AUSTRALIA.

"Thanks for driving," said Davnok.

"Sure thing," said Ben. "I love getting up at 5 a.m. to drive my brother to the airport."

"Hey-y-y," said Davnok, play-punching him.

"I'm just glad you're finally doing your master's degree,—after all these years,—so I can stop having to listen to you whine about it," said Ben.

"I've been planning for it,—methodically,—like a pro," said Davnok.

Ben chuckled.

"Yeah, yeah... whining," he said. "International law this, international law that. Blah, blah, blah."

"Uh-huh," said Davnok sarcastically, looking out the car window.

Ben drove up the ramp to the upper level of the airport terminal.

"More like scheming evil master plans," he said cheekily.

"More like working my ass off, living at Mom's, and saving seventy percent of my income for three years to afford this adventure, yeah," said Davnok proudly. "More like solid, premeditated planning, thank you very much."

"Mm-hmm, whatever you say," said Ben. He pulled up at the loading bay in front of the international departures entrance and jumped out to get Davnok's bags from the trunk: a duffel bag and a hiking pack. He placed them on the sidewalk at Davnok's feet and slammed the trunk shut. "Gotta run big brother," he said, hugging Davnok warmly. "Have fun."

"I will," said Davnok confidently.

"Oh, wait, wait, wait," said Ben. He reached into the car, pulled out a flat, wrapped present, and handed it to Davnok unceremoniously. "A little going-away present," he said, squeezing Davnok's shoulder. "Gotta beat the traffic back into the city, bye-e-e."

He jumped into the car and took off down the ramp.

II.

On the airplane, Davnok clipped in his seat belt and leaned back into his aisle seat with satisfaction. Other passengers shuffled up and down the aisles, shoved bags into overhead compartments, and waited patiently with impatience for others to get out of the way so they could climb into their seats. Davnok took the present out of his backpack and opened it carefully.

"Hmm," he smiled with closed lips.

"Is that *The Coffee Prince from Grenoble*?" said the older woman sitting next to him, peering curiously over the top of her spectacles.

"Ah, yeah, it's a French edition," said Davnok.

"Oh, how delightful," said the woman, smiling. "I just gave my grandson a copy of that book for his sixteenth birthday. Are you going on a quest like the Coffee Prince?"

"Ah," Davnok hesitated, "well, maybe... I guess every day's a coffee quest."

Ding. The lights flickered and the cabin crew manager began speaking on the intercom, welcoming passengers onboard.

"Anyway, don't mind me," said the woman courteously. She rummaged around in her handbag for a box of mints, popped one into her mouth, and smiled at him. "Enjoy your book."

"Thank you," said Davnok kindly.

The woman folded up her tray table and opened the in-flight magazine on her lap.

"Will my quest to find a decent boyfriend be successful?" thought Davnok.

III.

BERLIN, GERMANY. ONE AND A HALF YEARS LATER. Vanessa the C.I.A. operations officer opened the door as instructed and entered the windowless executive office suite.

"Good morning, ma'am," said Vanessa in her Texan accent.

"Good morning, Ms. Wong," said Clara the C.I.A. station chief. "Take a seat." She indicated the two chairs facing her desk.

"Thank you, ma'am," said Vanessa, taking the chair farthest from Clara.

"So we have a problem," said Clara impatiently. "We have a leak... the N.S.A. has a leak." Vanessa nodded seriously. "I've been informed that a German intelligence officer at the B.N.D.,—the Federal Intelligence Service,—gained unauthorized access to the selector lists and supporting documentation for the N.S.A.'s Hemispheric Ax program," said Clara.

"I see," said Vanessa. "I'm not aware of that program."

"This B.N.D. officer, Michael someone," said Clara, flipping through the printed file on her desk, "Michael Mittendorf. He called in and took leave from work this morning."

"Ah, that's not good," said Vanessa.

"No, it's not," said Clara. "I believe the words you're looking for are: 'oh, shit.' "

"Mm," Vanessa nodded.

"Hemispheric Ax has a code word-level security classification," said Clara. "Only a handful of our people know of its existence. The Germans were never supposed to know about it. We must prevent this disclosure."

"Yes, ma'am," said Vanessa. "Where is he?"

"We don't know," said Clara disapprovingly. "Here." She closed the file and slid it across the desk. Vanessa picked it up and flicked through it.

"Thank you, ma'am," she said.

"He has a son," said Clara. "There's nothing else in his life we can use."

"Okay," said Vanessa with a nod.

"This must be kept quiet," said Clara. "I don't want Langley breathing down my neck while I'm trying to stamp this fire out." She straightened her spine. "No unauthorized N.S.A. disclosures! Not while I'm station chief!" she said menacingly. "Take Simons and Matthews, I've reassigned them to you as team leader, effective immediately." She hunched forward. "Go and shut this thing down *now*!"

"Yes, ma'am," said Vanessa.

"The second you get a chance to grab Mittendorf, rendition him to Ramstein," said Clara. "We don't want him blabbing," she said, banging the desk with her hand.

"Yes, ma'am," said Vanessa.

"The second I get more information, I'll pass it along to you," said Clara. "You report directly to me."

"Yes, ma'am," said Vanessa.

"Get going," said Clara, waving her out of the office. "Shut this down *now*!"

IV.

STRASBOURG, FRANCE. Davnok followed Theo into the quickly filling lecture theater. They spotted their classmates in the back row and joined them.

"Happy Monday," said Hugo.

"Hi guys," said Juliette, Hugo's girlfriend.

"Happy Monday," said Davnok. "All ready for our final semester?"

"Yeah, you can say that again," said Juliette. "I've already got two internships lined up. Can't wait."

"Totally, I've had enough of exams," said Hugo. "I'm never doing another one again after this lot. Never again!" he said, raising a fist lightheartedly.

"Agreed," said Davnok. "I just hope I can get a full-time job again. My coffees don't pay for themselves."

"I'm just glad I never have to go back into politics," said Theo. "I'll be happy with a normal job in a normal office where I'm not surrounded by politicians and politician wannabes."

"Have you had Professor Vilchek before?" said Hugo to Theo.

"Not yet, this is my first class with him," said Theo. "You guys did though, right?"

"Yeah, he's pretty good," said Hugo.

"And he's not a know-it-all," said Davnok. "He's not as egotistical as some of the others."

Theo chuckled.

"Well that's nice to know," he said.

"Are you two coming to training tomorrow night?" said Hugo.

"You bet," said Davnok, looking to Theo.

"Yeah, I'm coming," said Theo.

"Great!" said Hugo. "We need——"

"Here he comes," said Juliette, tapping Hugo on the arm.

The professor walked into the lecture theater.

"He might play the chocolate game," said Davnok.

A hush descended upon the lecture theater.

"What's that?" whispered Theo.

"You'll just have to wait and see," whispered Davnok.

"Oh will I now?" whispered Theo playfully.

Hugo and Juliette glanced knowingly at each other. They had watched Davnok and Theo flirt shyly and politely for an entire semester.

*

With his head down, Professor Vilchek placed a stack of papers on the front bench and leaned on it with both hands. He exhaled, steeling himself for the beginning of another teaching semester, and looked up at the rows of student faces watching him intently.

"Good morning, everyone," he said with an existentially tired smile. "And welcome to our first lecture for this class: The United Nations and International Law. We are fortunate here in Strasbourg to be so close to one of the seats of the European Parliament: an important example of international treaty law in action. But today's lecture is about another of the principal international treaties in force in the world today: the Charter of the United Nations. Today, we are going to discuss some of the key facts about the structure of the General Assembly and the Security Council. I expect you all to have read the prescribed readings. Now, I have a bag of chocolates here: we're going to play a game of chocolate question time." Theo nudged Davnok with his knee and grinned. "Every correct answer earns a chocolate, and once you have earned a chocolate, you must stop answering questions and give your classmates an opportunity to earn one," said the professor. He tore the packet of individually wrapped chocolates open and held it up for all to see. "These are what you're playing for. Now, my first question is: What is the membership structure of the United Nations Security Council? Hmm? Who can tell me?"

A hand shot up.

"There are 15 members," said a student. "Made up of 10 rotating, non-permanent members, and 5 permanent members who are: China, France, Russia, the United Kingdom, and the United States."

"That is correct," said the professor. He lobbed a chocolate. The student caught it. "For simplicity, we shall refer to them as the 'Permanent Five,'" said the professor. "Now, next question: How are the rights of the Permanent Five different to the other members? Hmm?"

A hand shot up.

"The Permanent Five have veto power over Security Council resolutions," said a student.

"That is also correct," said the professor, lobbing a chocolate. "The Permanent Five have veto power. Each of them can block Security Council resolutions with a no vote." He paced around to the front of the bench. "Now, next question: What is the Security Council's main purpose? Hmm?"

A hand shot up.

"According to Article 24, paragraph 1 of the Charter, the Security Council has 'primary responsibility for the maintenance of international peace and security,'" said a student, reading from her notes.

"Correct," said the professor, lobbing a chocolate. "However," he raised a finger, "the Permanent Five can and do use their veto power to block Security Council resolutions that they don't like, even if such resolutions would increase international peace and security. Some of you may go on to work at the United Nations someday, and this is the politics you need to be aware of. The Permanent Five are the power brokers." He scratched his nose. "Okay, another chocolate question then: Who can tell me about the basic membership structure of the General Assembly? Hmm?"

A hand shot up.

"It's made up of all 193 United Nations member states," said a student. "They each have a single vote in the General Assembly."

"Yes," said the professor, lobbing a chocolate. "Now, somebody tell me: Can the General Assembly take actions relating to the maintenance of international peace and security? Hmm?"

A hand went up.

"No, sir," said a student. "Only the Security Council is mandated to do that."

"Very good," said the professor. "And this is a critically important point: the Security Council is the body that is mandated to take decisions related to armed conflict. The Security Council literally debates war." He lobbed a chocolate. "There is a rarely invoked, and strictly limited, technical exception to the rule of Security Council supremacy on such matters,—General Assembly resolution 377 A (V),—but otherwise, the General Assembly cannot take actions regarding the maintenance of international peace and security. It can only recommend that the Security Council consider a certain issue. It cannot compel the Security Council to consider that issue; or how to act on that issue. So," he clasped his hands together, "that's the basic structure of the General Assembly and the Security Council."

"Sir?" said a student.

"Yes?" said the professor.

"Why can't the General Assembly vote to change the veto system?" said the student.

"Good question, very good question," said the professor. "According to the Charter, resolutions on important matters,—such as amendments to the Charter,—must be passed by all 5 of the Permanent Five, *and* by the Security Council as a whole. In other words, any 1 of the Permanent Five can block any amendment to the Charter; even if all other member states want it to pass. The Permanent Five would almost certainly use their veto power to block any amendments that would limit their power. As you will have uncovered in your readings, the United Nations was created by the world powers at the end of World War II in 1945. It has retained essentially the same power structure since that time. If you want to deal with the United Nations on issues of international peace and security, you must deal with the Security Council and the Permanent Five, period."

Davnok frowned.

"Are the Permanent Five the reason the U.N. didn't stop the United States from invading Iraq?" he said.

Theo pressed his leg firmly against Davnok's leg. Davnok pretended not to notice.

"Well, how could it?" said the professor, shrugging. "How could any member state stop the United States from invading any country? It has the most powerful military in the world."

"Ah, I don't know," said Davnok.

"With or without Security Council resolutions," said the professor, hesitating, "*nota bene,*—note well,—my dear students: the United Nations is a formal forum for dispute resolution and cooperation between sovereign states. It is governed by a constitutional treaty: that's what the Charter is. Individual sovereign states are the highest legal authorities in the world. They are the creators of the United Nations, and its enforcers. The United Nations is not an international government. It is not an international parliament. It has no standing army. Only sovereign states themselves have the legal authority to enforce the law that emanates from the United Nations. And if no sovereign state is willing to challenge the actions of the United States, then its actions will go unchallenged."

Davnok leaned back in his chair and crossed his arms, perplexed.

"There is no international government," he thought; "it's a myth; it's just a chaotic international power hierarchy dominated by the United States through the arbitrary use of excessive force."

"Sir," said Davnok.

"Yes, Davnok?" said the professor.

"How can the U.N. make the world a more peaceful place if it can't stop the United States from invading and occupying which-ever states it wants?" said Davnok.

"Ah," the professor stuffed his hands into his pockets. "If it makes you feel any better, young man, you are not the first person to ask that question. Scholars, diplomats, politicians... many people have attempted to bring a more stable and lasting peace to the world. And," he hesitated, "well, let me say this: I do not believe more wars are the solution. Peace requires de-escalation of conflicts, not esca-lation. There is a whole academic field devoted to peace studies. But currently, the world is the way it is, young man. How are you going to restrain the United States government?" he said, display-ing his palms. "Even if the Security Council had somehow man-aged to pass a resolution banning the invasion of Iraq, the United States could still have invaded anyway. Who could have stopped them? But if you are going to work in international relations,—as some of you may well do,—you need to know how the United Nations is structured and how it functions."

The professor crossed his arms, changed the subject, and con-tinued the lecture.

*

Davnok looked down at his feet.

"He didn't answer my question" he thought. He glanced at Theo.

"So what then?" Davnok whispered in Theo's ear. "Are we just supposed to watch while the United States senselessly invades and murders and displaces millions of innocent people?" whispered Davnok.

"Maybe *you* can make a difference," whispered Theo surrepti-tiously.

"How could I possibly make the world listen to me?" whispered Davnok. "How could I make anybody listen to me? I'm nobody, I'm——"

The professor stopped speaking and looked up at them whispering.

"Shush," whispered Theo, nudging Davnok with his elbow.

V.

Davnok slotted coins into the old cafeteria coffee machine, pushed the buttons for black coffee and sugar, and watched the liquid spit out into a thin plastic cup with a splash and a hum. Students milled around plastic tables and chairs, gossiping and catching up, many for the first time since the Christmas holidays.

"Coffee should have milk," said Hugo jovially, waiting with his coins at the ready.

"Nah," said Davnok, grinning. "Coffee should be black."

"Coffee should have no sugar," said Hugo mockingly.

"No, no, no," said Davnok cheerfully. "I know when you're baiting me. And that's treasonous talk: there are laws against sugarless coffee, you know. It's illegal in fourteen countries," he joked, retrieving his coffee.

"You should ask Theo to dinner or something," said Hugo.

"Huh?" said Davnok, surprised. "Ask Theo to dinner? Where did that come from?"

"You two flirt like crazy," said Hugo.

"I didn't realize it was that obvious," said Davnok, embarrassed.

"Yeah, kind of," said Hugo. "Ask him out."

"No way," said Davnok, shaking his head.

"Yes way," said Hugo, nodding. "You're obviously into each other. You should do something about it."

"Almost every time I ask a guy out it's a complete disaster," said Davnok.

"Oh, it can't be that bad," said Hugo.

Davnok stared at him, unimpressed.

"Dating guys is a nightmare," said Davnok definitively. "Gee, how many times do I have to explain it to you? Why does nobody ever listen? Once they know I like guys, many guys will flirt and touch romantically, and lead me on emotionally. But when I get serious and ask them out for real, then they say they're straight. It's bullshit nonsense, but they don't have the *balls* to admit they like guys."

"Hey, don't get mad," said Hugo defensively.

"Why do you think I've never had a boyfriend?" said Davnok, frowning. "Most guys just want to play secretly and deny publicly. It's infuriating! I'm worth so much more than being treated like that. I'm boyfriend material!" he said, tapping himself on the chest.

"Yeah, but it's obvious he's into you," said Hugo.

"And did he say that?" said Davnok.

"Well, no, but I'm pretty sure he is," said Hugo.

"That's not the same thing," said Davnok, shaking his head. "He keeps talking about his ex-girlfriend. He's said nothing about liking guys... or liking me. And I'm not asking him. He'll deny it like they all do. I won't be the stupid fool who makes the first move; not again. I've been played too many times. If he doesn't have the balls to admit he's interested in me, then I'm not interested."

"The way you two were flirting in the lecture theater five minutes ago didn't look like you weren't interested," said Hugo.

"We're just friends," said Davnok, looking away.

"You message each other every single day," said Hugo.

"So what?" said Davnok.

Hugo sighed, slotted his coins into the coffee machine, and pressed the buttons. The machine hummed to life.

"Being around you two lately is like watching a drama series where two main characters are obviously destined to date from the first episode of the first season, but where it takes,—like,—seven seasons before they actually kiss or date or do something about it," he said.

"Hmm," grumbled Davnok.

"Really, man," said Hugo, putting a reassuring hand on Davnok's shoulder, "you can't hide this stuff. Not the way you two look at each other. Just ask him, it's very simple. And then I can win my beers."

"What does beer have to do with it?" said Davnok, scrunching up his face.

"Pierre bet me three beers that Theo would ask you out first," said Hugo. "I bet him you'd ask Theo out first. Thought it was an easy win."

Davnok snorted in amusement.

"I see," he said.

"So just ask him," said Hugo. "And then——"

"You're not going to win anything," said Davnok.

"Just ask him," said Hugo calmly. "And then you two can share a nice meal,—and stuff,—and I can win my beers. Anyway, aren't you supposed to be the——"

"I'm not going to ask him out just so you can win a beer," said Davnok, grinning awkwardly. "What do you think I——"

"What mischief are you two up to?" said Juliette, joining them by the coffee machine. "I sense a conspiracy."

"World peace," said Davnok quickly.

"Nothing," said Hugo, shaking his head.

"Yeah, right," said Juliette, not believing a word. "You told him, didn't you!' she said to Hugo.

"Told him what?" said Hugo innocently.

Juliette stared at him.

"I told you to let them be," said Juliette reproachfully.

Davnok sighed.

"Great, just great," he said. "Everybody's talking about it now." He blew on his coffee and tried to take a sip but it was too hot. "I've got study to do." He adjusted his backpack and headed toward the exit.

"Ask him!" called Hugo after him.

VI.

It was dark outside. Theo searched the study areas of the library and found Davnok tucked away in a nook on a cushioned bench with his feet up. His laptop rested on his athletic stomach and the light from the screen glowed on his face.

"I thought I might find you here," said Theo, taking a seat next to him.

"Hey," said Davnok, sitting up. He took off his headphones.

"So-o-o, what you up to?" said Theo.

"Looking at U.N. jobs," said Davnok.

"Cool, which ones?" said Theo.

"Here," said Davnok, handing him the laptop. "The problem is they want at least five years of experience in a relevant field before they'll even consider my application. And that's for an entry-level role."

"Yeah, I've heard that," said Theo, scrolling through the job listings.

"Even the administration officer roles require at least five years and a master's degree," said Davnok.

"Well you'll have your master's by the end of the semester," said Theo.

"Yeah, but I'll still only have three years of work experience," said Davnok.

"So you need a few more years' experience before you can work at the U.N.," said Theo with a shrug. "No big deal. That's not the end of the world."

"But what if it is?" said Davnok.

"I could introduce you to Professor Freyermuth if you like," said Theo.

"I expected to be doing something much more useful after this degree," grumbled Davnok. "I thought I'd be able to make a difference."

Theo nudged Davnok's leg with his knee. Davnok pretended not to notice.

"She might have some advice about internships," said Theo.

"I can't afford to do unpaid internships," said Davnok, annoyed. "I have rent and bills to pay. I don't have a choice, I have to get a job as soon as I graduate. Any job that pays. If I had to, I'd take one in the regional Russian city of Yakutsk where the temperature plummets to forty degrees below zero in winter. I really would."

"Oh, that might be a bit excessive," said Theo, grinning.

"I have to help make the world a more peaceful place," said Davnok passionately. "How can I do that if I'm just some admin guy doing everybody's errands and getting their coffee orders?"

"The stuff I did at the minister's office was mostly admin stuff," said Theo candidly. "It takes decades to gain any real authority."

"Yes, *I know*, but we don't have decades," said Davnok pressingly. "Our stupid heads of state could invade another innocent country tomorrow. They could start a nuclear war tomorrow. They damage our environment more and more every day. We need to get in there *now* to stop them!"

Theo pressed his knee against Davnok's leg and stared into his eyes, unblinking. Davnok swallowed hard with dread.

"Shit, he just wants to play," he thought. He moved his leg away and took back his laptop, like a tortoise retreating into its shell, and pretended to look at the screen. His heart beat in his ears and he blushed. "Don't look up," he thought; "don't look up, don't look up, don't look up." Unable to resist, he looked up. Theo stared ardently into his eyes and shifted closer, pressing his leg firmly against Davnok's leg. Davnok stared back, captivated and unable to look away from Theo's dilated pupils. "No, no, no," thought Davnok; "he doesn't want to date, he just wants to play."

"Ah," said Davnok, blanking. "Yeah," he said, packing his laptop and books into his backpack, preparing to leave.

"It takes time," said Theo hesitantly.

"Huh?" said Davnok, scrunching up his face.

"Never fear," said Theo.

"What?" said Davnok.

"Never mind," said Theo.

"Never mind what?" said Davnok.

"Nothing," said Theo.

"All right," said Davnok, looking away.

"I'm hungry," said Theo. "How about you? Would you like to go get some dinner?" He reached out and touched Davnok's hand.

"Now?" said Davnok, tingling with fear and excitement.

"Yeah," said Theo, nodding.

"Ah," Davnok wavered.

"Hamburgers, pizza, whatever," said Theo, putting his hand on Davnok's shoulder.

"Um, well, that's always tempting," said Davnok.

"Yeah, I know," said Theo.

Davnok pondered the invitation at length.

"Um, pizza maybe?" he said eventually.

"Cool, I know just the place," said Theo.

VII.

Davnok and Theo sat at a tiny table by a redbrick wall in an Italian restaurant, sipping red wine. Theo's leg was pressed firmly against Davnok's leg under the table. Davnok chuckled quietly.

"So-o-o, I suppose Pierre or Hugo put you up to this?" he said curiously.

"Put me up to what?" said Theo, cocking his head to one side.

"Never mind," said Davnok, smiling with closed lips.

"Did you finish reading the Giuseppe Tomasi di Lampedusa novel, *The Leopard*?" said Theo.

"Yeah, it was okay," said Davnok honestly.

Theo shrugged.

"I wish more people wrote like that these days," he said.

"You read a lot of classic literature," said Davnok.

"Yeah... I know," said Theo.

"I used to read a lot of classic literature, until a few years ago," said Davnok. "These days I prefer to read political stuff; and philosophical stuff." He paused. "Then again, doesn't Plato count as classic literature as well as philosophical?"

"Is there a political activist inside you bursting to get out?" said Theo inquisitively.

"Well, if I thought it'd be effective, I'd protest stuff, yeah," said Davnok. "But I'm not convinced that protesting achieves much."

"I disagree, I don't accept that," said Theo. "Protesting is important. Resistance is important. Governments and politicians must be held publicly accountable for their actions."

"But politicians don't listen," said Davnok, displaying his palms. "They don't care," he said, shaking his head. "If they did care, they wouldn't behave like greedy pigs. They just do whatever increases their personal wealth and power."

"I know," said Theo, nodding. "They don't represent or act for the public anymore; just for corporations and themselves."

"Australian politicians lie as if telling the truth were a crime," said Davnok. "They obstinately refuse to behave responsibly. They throw political power tantrums like spoiled toddlers, kicking and screaming. They're disgusting and disgraceful. Maybe I'll have to——"

The waiter approached and delivered their coffees and desserts. Davnok's hands darted to his coffee. Theo watched him perform his coffee ritual with amusement. Despite having witnessed it many times before, the novelty of it had yet to wear off. Davnok took a sachet of sugar in one hand and flicked it lightly so the sugar collected at the bottom. He tore off the top and carefully poured the contents into the steaming cup of black coffee in front of him. This he did twice more. He stirred gently,—both clockwise and anticlockwise,—until the crystals had dissolved, then replaced the teaspoon at the side of the saucer. But this was only half the ritual. Theo crossed his arms and watched with intrigue, despite knowing precisely what would happen next. Davnok folded two of the empty sachets lengthways in half and slid them neatly into the third. Nearly done, he folded the three torn-off tops of the sachets and slid them into the third sachet as well. When he was done, he folded and twisted the single resultant sachet into a Z-shape and placed it in the teaspoon at the side of the saucer. Then,—and only then,—did he begin to drink his coffee. He took a sip and looked at Theo with a shy flicker in his eye. He put down his coffee, picked up his dessert fork, carved off a mouthful of warm chocolate cake dripping with chocolate sauce, and ate it with pleasure. Theo stared deeply into his dark, striking eyes.

"Only heartless monsters drink black coffee," said Theo provocatively.

"Oh-h-h no, no way," said Davnok, grinning. "No, no, no. That's not how the legend goes. The coffee laws in *The Coffee Prince from Grenoble* are very clear. Law 1: Coffee must be made purely from roasted coffee beans. One who drinks impure coffee shall poison their mind. Law 2: Coffee must be black. One who drinks coffee with milk shall bleach their soul of all that is good. Law 3: Coffee must be sweetened with raw sugar. One who drinks coffee with no sugar shall kill the love in their heart."

"Did you memorize the whole novel?" said Theo, impressed.

"I can remember the coffee laws," said Davnok. "And the punishment for breaking them is self-executing: If one breaks all three coffee laws, one shall become an evil, soulless, and heartless monster. That's how it goes."

"And none of the gods have the power to reverse the punishment, if I remember correctly," said Theo.

Davnok nodded.

"That's right," he said. "Only heartless monsters can cure themselves with laborious labors of redemption. Anyway, you watched me add three sugars to my coffee, so I'm not a heartless monster."

"My ex-girlfriend used to quote that book all the time," said Theo.

Davnok raised an eyebrow.

"It is one of my favorites," he said.

"So let's play it forward then," said Theo. "Does that mean that if you cut back from three sugars to one sugar, you'd be more heartless than you are now?"

Davnok chuckled.

"Not really, no," he said. "That's not how I understand it. The way I interpret it, you either have sugar or you don't. And if you don't, *then* you'll become heartless."

"I suspect you would've made a good lawyer back in Melbourne," said Theo.

"That's not what I want to do," said Davnok. He carved off a mouthful of chocolate cake and ate it.

"So what were you saying before dessert arrived?" said Theo. "I get the impression you want to be a politician one day."

"Well, honestly, I don't want to be a politician... or a public figure," said Davnok, carefully considering his words. He paused and contemplated the masonry of the redbrick wall beside them. "I'd detest the publicity. Fame's a curse. If I truly thought becoming a politician could help fix the corruption, I'd do it,—I have considered it,—but I'm not sure it'd make much difference. I think I can do more good as a non-politician."

"Good people should run for office, whatever their background, wherever they are, and at every level of government," said Theo.

"But you're a good person and you don't want to be a politician," said Davnok, shrugging.

"Wouldn't do it if you put a gun to my head," said Theo. "It's horrible."

"And there's the catch," said Davnok knowingly.

"So you're aiming at the U.N. instead," said Theo.

"Yeah, thought it was the best place to make a difference," said Davnok. "But I'm not so sure anymore. And I have to start submitting job applications soon."

He ate the remaining mouthfuls of chocolate cake. Theo finished his ice cream and set down his spoon.

"Yeah, I'm not sure what the solution is either," he said. "But that was delicious."

"Mine was too," said Davnok. "Would you like to go for a walk... to burn off these heavy desserts?"

"Yeah, I'd like that," said Theo. "And who in their right mind would say no to an after-dinner walk with the Coffee Prince of Strasbourg?"

Davnok chuckled.

"Oh, nonsense," he said, grinning from ear to ear.

VIII.

It was cold outside. The stars above shone clear and bright. Davnok looped his arm around Theo's arm and shoved his hand into his warm jacket pocket, locking their arms together. They passed the charming canals and bridges in the old district of Petite France and walked contentedly through the flat streets in the direction of the university. Their shoulders bumped gently as they went, gravitating closer and closer with each step.

"Should I kiss him now?" thought Davnok.

"They started laying the foundations in A.D. 1015, you know," said Theo, gazing at the illuminated spire of the Notre-Dame Cathedral of Strasbourg.

"Really?" said Davnok. "That's ancient."

"Yeah, a thousand years old... give or take," said Theo. "I think it was——"

Suddenly, unable to resist the urge any longer, Davnok took his hand out of his pocket and pulled Theo's slim body into his arms. Theo's face lit up with surprise and he put his hands lightly around Davnok's waist and stared into his eyes.

"Kiss him now," thought Davnok. He leaned in.

Without warning, they were both grabbed by the arms and dragged into an alleyway.

"Urgh!" grunted Theo.

"Hey!" shouted Davnok. "What do——" He was punched in the face and pummeled to the ground. Someone held his arm awkwardly behind his back and kneed him in the spine. His cheek was pushed flat against the cold cobblestones. He looked across to see Theo beside him, pinned down in the same position. A figure in dark clothes and a balaclava was kneeing him in the back. "Are you okay?" said Davnok.

"Shut up!" said a woman harshly.

The person holding Davnok's arm twisted it further in the direction of pain.

"Argh!" winced Davnok.

The woman's feet stepped into view. She knelt down,—her face hidden behind a balaclava,—and held a gun to Theo's temple.

"Your father stole highly classified information from the N.S.A.," said the woman in an American accent.

"I don't know what——" said Theo, grunting.

"Shut it," snapped the woman.

She pressed the cold muzzle of her gun harder against his temple. With her free hand she pulled up his jacket, exposed his stomach, and jammed her gloved fingers under the side of his rib cage.

"Urgh!" groaned Theo, wrenching involuntarily.

"Don't waste my time, or yours, Theo Mittendorf," she said. "Your father stole a selector list and other documentation from an N.S.A. program. He intends to leak it. Now, I don't know where he is. But I do know exactly who he is. I know exactly who you are. And I know exactly who your boyfriend Davnok is." She looked at Davnok. "We know everything about you," she said, holstering her gun. "So let me make this clear and simple," she looked to Theo, "and let me be honest: I like honesty. I'm taking Davnok. And if your father leaks a single selector,—a single name, a single I.P. address, a single email address, a single phone number,—from that list, or any other program information, then I will kill your boyfriend. You will never see or hear from him again. And then I'll kill you. Wherever you are, wherever you hide, I will find you and make your death look like an accident. We learned our lessons about leakers the hard way with Edward Snowden and Chelsea Manning, and——"

"Theo, what's going on?" said Davnok with exasperation.

"Shut up," said the woman. Davnok's attacker punched him in the side. "If you want to know what happens to leakers under the Hawk administration, look at what happened to Indira Chandra in Mumbai," said the woman to Theo. "Look it up," she said flippantly. "Stop the leak immediately or die. The choice is yours." She stood up. "Wind him," she said to Theo's attacker.

Theo was rolled onto his side and punched hard upward into his stomach. He heaved and groaned and tried to suck in short breaths.

"Go to hell!" shouted Davnok.

He was punched repeatedly into silence.

"Davnok!" gasped Theo, trying to shout with empty lungs. "Davnok!"

He rolled onto his back, trying to breathe. The attackers disappeared stealthily into the night. Theo rolled onto his side and looked around, gasping. Davnok was gone. Theo groaned and

The Cathedral of Strasbourg (c. 1876).

wrapped his arms around himself. The dampness of the street crept into his bones. For minutes, he lay there catching his breath. Eventually, his breathing stabilized. He stood up gingerly and stretched his back.

"How the hell do I get Davnok back?" he thought.

He rested his hands on his knees and focused on the ground.

IX.

Theo banged loudly on the apartment door.

"It's me, it's Theo, let me in!" he called urgently.

"Stop banging," said a voice from inside. The lock turned and the door opened to reveal Hugo looking tired and scruffy. "What's going on, man?"

Theo shoved his way past him and slammed the door shut.

"Bolt it, lock it, make sure it's locked," he said tensely. "Don't let anybody in. Nobody. Do you understand?"

"Man, are you okay?" said Hugo, bewildered. "You've got a swollen eye." Theo hurried to Davnok's bedroom, switched on the light, and paced back and forth with his hands on his head, muttering to himself. "He's not here," said Hugo.

Theo huffed.

"I know he's not here!" he shouted.

"Huh?" said Hugo.

In the living room, Juliette paused the show she and Hugo were watching and joined Hugo in the hallway.

"Theo, is everything all right?" she said.

"No!" said Theo.

He stormed out of the bedroom, took Hugo and Juliette's devices without explanation, tossed them into the freezer,—along with his own device,—and herded Hugo and Juliette into the apartment's small bathroom.

"Man, what's going on with you?" said Hugo.

Theo closed the bathroom door and turned on the shower and the exhaust fan.

"They took Davnok!" he whispered urgently.

"What do you mean '*took*'?" whispered Juliette with alarm.

"Who's they?" whispered Hugo. "Why are we whispering?"

"The Americans, the N.S.A., the C.I.A.,... whichever blasted agency does their illegal work in France and Germany," said Theo. "They attacked us in the street and abducted him!"

"What?" said Hugo frantically.

"Yeah," said Theo, rubbing his swollen eye and wincing. "They said they'd kill Davnok if I didn't stop my father from blowing the whistle on an N.S.A. program."

"Is your father a spy?" said Juliette interrogatively.

"No," said Theo, shaking his head. "He's an infrastructure analyst with the German food and agriculture ministry. But that's not the——"

"What does he have to do with the N.S.A.?" said Hugo, frowning.

"Why is he blowing the whistle?" said Juliette.

"Is this,—like,—an Edward Snowden thing?" said Hugo.

"I don't know, maybe," said Theo, shrugging restlessly.

"Shit," said Juliette.

"What about Davnok?" said Hugo. "We have to go to the police."

"Absolutely not!" said Theo. "The French government will side with the American government and the N.S.A.!" he said, throwing his hands up. "We can't trust the government!"

"Well, maybe not the American government; but we can trust the French government, and the French police," said Juliette.

"Bullshit!" said Theo. "They're all part of the American empire. They won't help us, and they can't protect us from the Americans."

"But how can we save Davnok?" said Hugo, terrified. "We have to stop your father from publicizing whatever this N.S.A. thing is."

"Did your father steal N.S.A. information?" said Juliette.

"I don't know," said Theo dismissively. "But I know,—I'm sure,— that whatever he's doing, he's doing the right thing. He's a responsible person. If he's blowing the whistle, then the whistle needs to be blown," he said adamantly.

"But you just said the Americans will kill Davnok if he blows the whistle," said Hugo.

"I know, I know," said Theo. "But even if I did try to stop my father, it wouldn't make Davnok any safer. They might just kill him anyway. They wouldn't want him talking about being abducted by the C.I.A., would they? And if I lead them to my father, they'll certainly kill *him*. He's the one they want to silence."

"How do you know all this?" said Juliette.

Theo sighed.

"The woman," he said. "Our attacker. She said if I didn't cooperate, then my fate would be the same as Indira Chandra who——"

"Who's Indira Chandra?" said Hugo.

Theo exhaled loudly.

"Indira Chandra was killed for attempting to expose an N.S.A. surveillance program in India last year," he said. "She made contact with a journalist from the *Times of India* but was shot dead in the street in Mumbai by a sniper,—in broad daylight,—before she could hand over her trove of documents proving N.S.A. surveillance and C.I.A. blackmail of Indian government politicians. The only reason we know about it is because that journalist reported what Chandra had told him before she was assassinated, even though he didn't have any evidence and couldn't prove United States government involvement. It wasn't reported outside of India,—the story wasn't picked up by the empire-friendly news media in English-speaking countries,—but people in the international intelligence community noticed it. My father noticed it."

"I thought you said your father's not a spy," said Juliette suspiciously.

"He's not!" said Theo unequivocally.

"But——" said Juliette.

"Look, the threat's real," said Theo. "Once the Americans get what they want, they'll probably kill us off to shut down the story; to stop any leak from getting out. They're scrambling. They're trying to intimidate us."

"They *are* intimidating us!" exclaimed Juliette.

"They think I'll just cower and obey their threats," said Theo. "But I think we need to get out in front of this. Control the narrative, control the game."

"Huh?" said Hugo, baffled.

"The golden rule of political communication," said Theo. "We have to be the ones to set the narrative. We have to go public. It's the only thing that can save Davnok, and me, and my father; if anything can. The only strategy that can defeat government secrecy is public exposure."

"That's insane!" said Juliette. "You have to do what they want! They've got Davnok!"

"Man, I think she's right," said Hugo. "You have to stop your father; or go to the police."

"Bullshit!" said Theo, getting redder in the face. "The only way out of this is offense. If we give in to their demands, they'll probably just kill us."

"Hey, you put us in danger by coming here," said Hugo unsympathetically.

"This was the closest place to go," said Theo defensively. "I had to get off the street. And I trust you two. I thought I'd be safe here." Juliette stared at him uneasily. "Fine," said Theo. He pushed his way out of the bathroom and retrieved his device from the freezer. "I know what I have to do."

Juliette and Hugo stepped out of the bathroom and gave each other puzzled looks. Theo went back into the bathroom, locked the door, and sat on the edge of the bathtub with his device at the ready. He looked in the mirror and quickly ran a hand through his wavy hair to neaten it.

"It doesn't matter," he thought.

He took a deep breath, held his device out in front of him to capture his face and upper body, and pressed record, streaming live to his primary social media account.

"I'm Theo Mittendorf," he said clearly. "I'm German. My father is Michael Mittendorf: a German government employee. He was going to blow the whistle on an N.S.A. surveillance program." He looked at his watch. "About fifteen minutes ago, my boyfriend and I were attacked and beaten in Strasbourg by three people wearing balaclavas——"

"Theo!" shouted Juliette, banging on the bathroom door. "What are you doing? Stop! They'll kill him!"

Theo looked resolutely at the camera.

"They abducted my boyfriend, Davnok Willinger: an Australian," he said. "One of the attackers,—a woman with a perfect American accent,—threatened to kill Davnok if I didn't stop my father from blowing the whistle. They——"

"He's streaming it live!" said Hugo, panicking. "Stop!" he shouted, banging on the bathroom door. "Stop, Theo! Stop streaming! They'll kill him!" He banged harder. "Theo!" he shouted. "Stop it right now!"

Theo ignored the noise and focused on the camera.

"The woman also threatened to kill me if my father blew the whistle," he said firmly, his veins pulsing with adrenaline. "I believe they're trying to intimidate me into contacting my father so they can locate and kill him, just like they assassinated Indira Chandra in

India last year for attempting to blow the whistle on N.S.A. surveillance and C.I.A. blackmail of Indian government politicians——"

"Stop streaming!" shouted Hugo. "They'll kill him! You've lost your mind!"

Theo kept his eyes on the camera.

"If Davnok Willinger is killed or disappeared; if I'm killed or disappeared; if Michael Mittendorf is killed or disappeared,—under any circumstances,—then, I'm telling you right now, it will be the Americans who did it," he said emphatically. "Do it father! Blow the whistle! Do it for German democracy!"

"Theo!" shouted Hugo hysterically, banging on the door.

"The world has had enough of United States government terrorism!" declared Theo darkly. "The United States government needs to *back off* and stop intruding in places it doesn't belong!"

He ended the recording and unlocked the door. Hugo and Juliette stared furious daggers at him.

"You just killed him!" shouted Hugo.

"No!" said Theo. "I just saved his life, most likely. And my life; and my father's life. The Americans want to silence us. If I did what they want, there's no guarantee they wouldn't kill Davnok anyway. I just saved us."

"You have to delete the video right now, before it gets out!" said Juliette.

"Absolutely not," said Theo.

"Give me the device," demanded Hugo.

"No," said Theo, walking past him into the living room.

"Here, give it!" demanded Hugo, grabbing him in a headlock.

Theo grunted and dropped his device. He moved his body in closer to Hugo's center of gravity, punched him hard in the groin, whipped his other arm around the front of Hugo's face, and slammed him hard to the floor. He quickly retrieved his device before Juliette could pick it up. Hugo lay on the floor clutching his groin, groaning. Theo stood with his back to the wall and quickly searched the contact details for the *Intercept*, *Mediapart*, and the *Guardian*, and forwarded copies of his video with a brief and alarming message subject line that he hoped would get their attention. Juliette crossed her arms and scowled at him.

"I'm calling the police," said Juliette caustically.

Without a word, Theo stalked out the front door and slammed it shut behind him.

X.

GENEVA, SWITZERLAND. Michael stared blankly out the hotel room window and frowned. The placid waters of Lake Geneva glimmered in the moonlight chill. He crossed his arms and turned to look at the two journalists sitting around the low coffee table, one on the couch, and the other on the armchair beside it. They were hunched over their laptops, surrounded by empty room service trays and tea and coffee cups. A wall-mounted television screen flickered mutely, displaying B.B.C. News.

"Are you ready to continue with the interview?" said Tarik the *Intercept* journalist in his London accent.

"Sure," said Michael.

He took a seat in an armchair in the corner of the room, facing a video camera and light boxes.

"Great," said Tarik.

He got up from the couch and switched on the light boxes.

"Ah, guys," said Henry the *Intercept* journalist, scrutinizing his screen. He took off his headphones. "I think you need to take a look at this."

He turned his laptop to face them and played Theo's video.

"Oh, shit," said Michael, sighing heavily.

He brought a hand defensively to his neck and watched in terror to the end.

"Well, at least he supports you," said Tarik. "I mean, he told you to blow the whistle, right?"

Michael held his hands up.

"Stop, stop, stop, halt everything!" he said. "No publication," he said, shaking his head vigorously. "Do not publish a word of Hemispheric Ax. Neither of you is to publish a single word." He glared at them. "Not you, not your editors, nobody," he said, inhaling and exhaling loudly with vexed puffs.

"We won't publish without your approval," said Tarik deferentially. "But Theo's given you his approval. And if the Americans hurt him or his boyfriend now, there'll be a public backlash. The video's a clever move."

"I didn't think my actions would put him in this kind of danger," said Michael, massaging his brow. "I knew they'd come after me,

I knew they might put him under surveillance; but I didn't think they'd threaten him. And abduction. This is insane! This changes everything!" he said, waving at the camera and light boxes. "I have to go and mitigate these threats before we can publish."

"What?" said Henry with alarm.

"How?" said Tarik, puzzled.

"We can't risk publishing while my son's being threatened with assassination and this new boyfriend is being held hostage," said Michael apprehensively.

"Okay, that's one thing," said Tarik, controlling his composure, "but you can't go out in public now. You'll expose yourself. You'll risk everything. You'll already be on every law enforcement watch list in Germany. And now that this video is out there, the whole world will know your name within a day, Michael. That's why we came here: to shield you for as long as possible while we publish. That's why the hotel booking is under Henry's name. Nobody else knows you're here. That was the whole point. You know what the Americans will do to you if they catch you," he said warningly.

"Yeah, they'll blow my brains out," said Michael. "Just like Indira Chandra."

"That's what I'm afraid of," said Tarik. "How could you possibly mitigate threats like that?"

"I can't tell you," said Michael. "I have to contact some people. But I can't risk using electronic communication. It's too late for all that; it's all compromised. I'd be traced here, and my contacts would be traced and silenced too. Ancient, in-person, face-to-face communication is the only reasonably secure way to communicate now; despite all the risks it carries."

"Hmm," grumbled Tarik.

"I miscalculated their reaction," said Michael regretfully. "We can deal with publication once my Theo is safe."

"But the Bolivian foreign relations minister is coming tomorrow to discuss asylum," said Tarik imploringly.

"I know, I know," said Michael, losing patience. "He'll just have to wait. There's no way around this. My son is my son. I'll be back as soon as I can. Or I'll send a cutout,—a courier,—to give you instructions. Just don't publish anything until I give the all clear." He headed hastily to the door. "Theo is the reason I'm blowing the whistle. I want him to live in a free and democratic Germany; not one dominated by the Americans."

He clenched his jaw.

"Michael," said Tarik pleadingly, "I don't want you to become another Indira Chandra. Please, there has to be another way. *Please* reconsider."

"If I can't come," said Michael, putting a hand on the door handle, "I'll send a cutout to give you my instructions using the paroles,—the passphrases,—I taught you. If someone comes to you,—allegedly on my behalf,—and they can't answer the paroles, then tell them to go to hell."

"All right," said Tarik grudgingly.

"Watch your back," said Henry with pity.

"I'll be as careful as I can, but I have to protect my son," said Michael, frowning. "I will not sacrifice him for this." He turned on his heels, yanked open the heavy door, and stormed out. "I hoped to keep him out of this deranged world of espionage!" he called over his shoulder, as the door slammed shut with a resounding thud.

XI.

STRASBOURG, FRANCE. Pierre switched off the boiling kettle at the power point and poured the steaming water into a coffee plunger; the ground coffee sloshed around like a whirlpool. He carried it into the living room in his tiny student apartment and placed it carefully on the coffee table as Theo finished telling his story.

"I just hope Davnok's okay," said Theo, sighing. "I would,— like,—die if something happened to him because of me."

"I hope he's okay too," said Pierre, taking a seat uneasily on the edge of the couch. "It's just terrible."

"I wish my father would blow the whistle already so this can all be over," said Theo.

"Did he tell you about what he's doing?" said Pierre.

"No," said Theo, shaking his head. "I don't know anything. I wish——"

Bing. The doorbell rang. They stared at each other with wide eyes.

"I'm not expecting anybody," said Pierre in a whisper.

"I didn't tell anybody I'm here," said Theo. "Juliette might have suspected I'd come here but..."

"Maybe they'll just go away," said Pierre. Theo crossed his arms. Bing. The doorbell rang again. "Let's just wait and see if they go away," said Pierre.

Bing. Bing. The doorbell continued to ring. For five awkward minutes, they sat and waited, trying to ignore it.

"Maybe we should——" said Theo.

"But we don't know who it is," said Pierre. "What if it's the Americans? What if they retaliate for your video?"

"If it was the Americans, they'd have kicked the door down with guns blazing already," said Theo. Bing. Bing. The doorbell continued to ring. "Clearly whoever it is isn't going away," said Theo. "Please just see who it is."

"Fine," said Pierre, getting up to answer the intercom. "Hello?"

"Good evening," said a man in a serious voice. "It's Mr. Monfils here, I'm an intelligence officer with the D.G.S.I.,—the General Directorate of Internal Security,—I'm here with a colleague. We're looking for Theo Mittendorf. We would like to speak with him, please."

"Haw, shit," guffawed Pierre in disbelief. He slapped a hand over his mouth, took his finger off the intercom, and looked at Theo. "I can't believe it. For real. French intelligence is knocking on my door!"

"Hmm, I don't like this," muttered Theo.

"Look man," said Pierre, "I don't trust the government any more than you do, but it's very hard for me to tell the D.G.S.I. to go away."

"Hmm," grumbled Theo.

"I kind of have to let them in," said Pierre, shrugging.

"But they can't do anything," said Theo. "What are they going to do? They can't protect me from the Americans. They just want to find my father, I bet you anything."

"I can't lie to them," said Pierre. "They must already know you're here. How else would they know to come here?"

Theo huffed and hauled himself off the couch.

"Good evening, officer, this is he," he spoke into the intercom. "May I ask what this is about?"

"May we come up to speak with you, please?" said the officer.

"May I kindly ask what you wish to speak with me about, officer?" said Theo.

Pierre crossed his arms.

"I would rather speak with you in person, Mr. Mittendorf," said the officer. "It is a matter of national security." He hesitated. "We would like to speak with you about the video you posted this evening."

Theo took his finger off the intercom.

"I told you," he said to Pierre. "These guys just want to get to my father. They're not here to help me, or Davnok."

"I have to let them in," said Pierre. "I'll try to protect you,—you're welcome to stay,—but I can't say no to the D.G.S.I. And besides, maybe they can help you. Who knows?"

Theo closed his eyes and nodded reluctantly.

"Okay," he said. "But we need a safety net."

"Like what?" said Pierre.

"I'm going to stand in the doorway and ask them to stay out in the corridor," said Theo. "I want you to record me while I talk to them,—stream it live from your device,—so if anything happens to me, there'll be public evidence. These guys break all the laws and all the rules. They're dangerous and they're not on our side."

"Is that really a good idea?" said Pierre skeptically.

"Can you just record me please?" said Theo.

"Okay, okay," said Pierre.

"Come on up, officer," said Theo, holding his finger on the intercom. "Second floor, first door on the left." He buzzed the officers into the building, opened the apartment door a crack, and blocked it from opening further with his foot. "Start recording me," he whispered to Pierre.

Pierre stood out of sight from the corridor and started recording. Dressed in casual business wear, the two officers came up the stairs.

"Good evening," said the older of the two officers at the door, unsmiling.

He produced identification and introduced himself. The younger officer stood silently next to him.

"My friend is recording us and streaming live," said Theo to the older officer, keeping his foot against the door.

"Then perhaps," said the officer, taking half a step back, "we will stay out here on your doorstep. It would be best if our faces were not recorded or displayed in the media."

"Sure," said Theo, keeping his body behind the door.

"We have been asked by our German law enforcement counterparts to speak with you," said the officer. "We're concerned that your father intends to leak secret government information that could damage French and German security. We are... assisting our German partner service in this matter as we,—of course,—have jurisdiction over all domestic security matters in France."

"Okay," said Theo evenly.

"When did you last communicate with your father?" said the officer.

"I saw him at Christmas," said Theo. "I haven't seen him since then."

"Do you know where he is currently?" said the officer interrogatively.

"The last I heard he was still in Frankfurt am Main," said Theo.

"Do you have any secret government information in your possession?" said the officer.

"Absolutely not," said Theo sternly, shaking his head.

"Do you know what secret information your father,—allegedly,—has in his possession?" said the officer.

"No, I do not," said Theo firmly. "All I know is what the American woman told me when they attacked me and my friend."

"I need to be careful," thought Theo; "I better not get tangled up in a web of allegations with the D.G.S.I."

"Do you——" said the officer.

"I don't know what my father might know," said Theo. "He's just an infrastructure analyst with the German food and agriculture ministry. I don't know how he could possibly have any N.S.A. information. But I do know that the N.S.A. should not be in Germany. The N.S.A. does not belong in my country, and our intelligence services should not be cooperating with it. If my father somehow has evidence of N.S.A. activity in Germany, then yeah, he should totally blow the whistle. And I'm totally within my rights to think that." He looked the officer directly in the eyes. "I believe strongly in the independence of my country. As you,—surely,—believe in the political independence of your country, officer."

"I see," said the officer guardedly.

The younger officer blushed with shame.

"Can you help me rescue my friend?" said Theo to the older officer. "Can you protect me?"

"Oh, well... what do you mean?" said the older officer evasively.

"Can you put me under police protection so the Americans can't attack me again?" said Theo. "Can you help rescue my friend?"

"Oh, I don't think the Americans would dare operate on French soil in the way you described in your video," said the officer dismissively. "I think,—perhaps,—you may have been exaggerating on that particular point. The United States is,—naturally,—a French ally. And allies don't spy on each other, as a rule. And our security services are very good here in France,—of course,—the best in the world. And we are very good at detecting and deporting foreign spies. France is a strong, independent, democratic republic. The Americans know better than to interfere in France. They wouldn't do that."

Standing out of sight, Pierre's jaw dropped.

"The Americans abducted my friend and threatened to kill us if I didn't stop my father from blowing the whistle," said Theo sternly. "I'm not lying! Why would I make that up?"

"I don't know why, but I think it must be an exaggeration," said the officer. "I don't believe the Americans would do that. Have you been drinking or taking illicit substances today?"

The younger officer pursed his lips. His eyes said that he believed Theo, but his mouth remained silent. Theo frowned crossly.

"No," he said curtly. "I have not been *drinking*."

The older officer leaned to one side and almost tried to peer around the door but thought better of it and stopped himself. The mere possibility of being recorded put him off-balance.

"In any event, locating your father is a matter of French and German security," he said. "You are,—of course,—welcome to report your alleged assault to the police," he said loudly, for the benefit of any recording. "French law enforcement and security services are here to protect French and European citizens. We are at your disposal." He straightened his back. "Please, contact me immediately if your father makes contact with you. We're here to help."

He offered his business card.

"Sure," said Theo impassively. "Thank you kindly, gentlemen, for your visit." He took the business card. "And have a pleasant evening."

He closed the door firmly and locked it before the officer had a chance to say anything more.

"Wow," said Pierre. He stopped recording and slumped onto the couch. "They don't care about Davnok's abduction at all. They don't want to know about it."

Theo eased himself onto the couch and rubbed his temples.

"They're just looking out for themselves," he said. "The glorious D.G.S.I. and its precious relationship with the B.N.D. They're all part of the empire. What do they care about a few pesky civilians?"

"But Davnok!" exclaimed Pierre.

"I know," said Theo, his eyes beginning to water. "I know." He covered his face with his hands. "It's madness," he muttered under his breath.

"But what can we do?" said Pierre, sitting upright.

"All we can do is wait for my father to blow the whistle," said Theo. "And hope that——"

"Hope?" said Pierre. "Hope? What good does hope do while Davnok's out there, somewhere, being held hostage by the Americans!"

Theo sighed.

"I don't know right now," he said.

"What's your father waiting for?" said Pierre, scrolling through the newsfeeds on his device. "Why hasn't he blown the whistle already? What's he waiting for?"

"I——" said Theo.

"Look," said Pierre, holding up his device, "your story is the top story on the *Intercept*'s main page. It's out there, your story's out there. What's he waiting for?"

"I don't know," said Theo. He looked to the window as if it might somehow reveal the answer. "I thought he would've done it by now."

"I think you know more than you're letting on," said Pierre suggestively.

Theo stared at him gravely but said nothing.

XII.

Sitting in a parked car, shrouded in darkness, watching Pierre's apartment windows from a distance, Vanessa held her device to her ear and let Clara's abuse flow around her.

"This is all *your* fault!" hissed Clara. "The media are already running the story. Now you have to maintain your distance! Publicity is the last thing I want!"

"It's not my fault," thought Vanessa; "I did exactly the same as last time."

"I'll keep him under surveillance," she said consolingly.

"Don't touch the son, but yes, keep a close watch," said Clara. "You still have to find Mittendorf. Is that understood?"

"Yes, ma'am," said Vanessa.

"It's getting more involved by the hour," said Clara with discontent. "The ambassador is involved now. The Germans have agreed to extradite Mittendorf to the U.S. if he's arrested. That's the last thing I want!"

"Understood," said Vanessa.

"Find him before the Germans do, before anybody else does," said Clara commandingly. "We don't want him talking!"

"Yes, ma'am," said Vanessa.

"And who's got the boyfriend now?" said Clara.

"Simons is holding him," said Vanessa. "The Munich team will be here in a few hours to collect him."

"Good," snapped Clara, ending the call.

*

Vanessa sighed and looked at her daypack on the passenger seat. Her cigarettes were right there, beckoning: the health warning in black and white, the friendly logo, the tastefully colored graphics and borders. She flipped the pack open, slipped a cigarette between her lips, and lit up, blowing a plume of smoke over the steering wheel.

"I'll find you, Mittendorf," she thought tranquilly; "you won't know what hit you."

XIII.

A man in a black balaclava hauled Davnok roughly upright, removed the soaking gag from his mouth, and let him choke and cough up water and splutter for air. Davnok's hands and feet were bound, he was blindfolded, his face was swollen, and his cut lip stung.

"I don't know anything!" he cried out desperately. "Why don't you believe me?" The man didn't respond. "Make it stop," whimpered Davnok, slumping onto the concrete floor, defeated and gasping for breath. "Plea-a-a-se make it stop."

"When did they move me to this room?" he thought wildly.

He squinted through a thin gap in the blindfold and tried to look about. There was a door that appeared to be made of metal. Clang. It opened and the feet of another person walked in.

XIV.

FRANKFURT AM MAIN, GERMANY. TWO DAYS LATER. Karsten the B.N.D. counterterrorism director left the situation room with his leather document folder under an arm and returned,—along the stark corridors,—to his office: a small and conspicuously neat room at the B.N.D.'s secret headquarters. He ran a hand through his thinning and graying blond hair.

"What a day," he thought.

He closed his eyes and exhaled stress. It was late. It had been twelve long hours since his work day had begun. He grabbed his scarf, coat, and satchel, and left the office.

*

In a trance of fatigue, the tedious drive home passed unnoticed, and he arrived in his driveway with a worn-out sigh.

"Finally, I can have some food and sleep," he thought.

His eyelids were heavy. He walked up the walkway to the front door. The porch light came on automatically and he dropped his satchel in fright at what he saw.

"Oh, no," he said under his breath. "Oh, no."

"I'm in it now," he thought; "now there's no avoiding it." There, at the foot of the front door to his idyllic little house in the suburbs of Frankfurt, were three small Xs marked in white chalk, arranged in a pyramid. A calling card from none other than Michael Mittendorf: the signal they had agreed upon over thirty years before. "I must be hallucinating," thought Karsten. He rubbed his eyes and looked again: Michael's chalk marks were still there, unmistakable. "Blast," he thought. The chalk marks signaled the need to meet at a secret location the following day at midday; and failing that, the day after, and so on until contact was made, or until a dead drop spike was planted at the secret location with a handwritten message inside as an alternative form of communication. "This has to be about the N.S.A.," he thought. He had seen the report in the *Intercept*. He had seen Theo's video. The whole of the B.N.D. was abuzz with surreptitious gossip and rumors about it. But until now,

Karsten had not been involved. He knew Michael was discontented with the escalating integration of the B.N.D. with the N.S.A. Many insiders were uncomfortable with it; many of them had noticed the warning signs: the breaches of interagency protocols, procedures, and information sharing. But going public with N.S.A. information was a momentous act of defiance. And now Michael had reached out and contacted him. "Now I'm involved," he thought. Now a line could be drawn directly from Theo to Michael to him. A very dangerous line. Karsten's shoulders sank.

"Michael blasted Mittendorf," he said quietly. A headache formed in his temples, like a storm that appears abruptly without warning. He had never believed this day would come. It wasn't his job to get involved, he had told himself. It was the job of the parliament and the chancellery, he had told himself. But deep down he knew they were doing all the wrong things for all the wrong reasons. And every year, it was getting worse. He groaned, unlocked the front door, and went inside. He undressed, got into the shower, and leaned his head against the shower screen glass with the steam rising around him and the water hitting the back of his neck, wishing all his troubles would disappear down the drain. "Michael, Michael, Michael," he said softly.

"You're trying to do the right thing," he thought; "but you can't do it on your own, and it'll take many more than two of us to do what needs to be done."

XV.

POTSDAM, GERMANY. THE NEXT MORNING. The peaceful and picturesque city,—covered in a very thin layer of snow,—would usually have calmed Karsten's nerves. Usually, it would have reminded him of childhood vacations. But the sights and sounds were not peaceful and picturesque enough to drown out the anxiety he carried within. He parked his car on the periphery and walked into the old town center with the bent-over posture of a slave about to be beaten. Had he not been so distracted, he would have been happy to take an interest in the streets and tram lines he knew well. Had he not been so distracted, he would have been happy to browse in his favorite Potsdam bookstore. But he was too distracted, and he barely noticed anything. He turned down

Brandenburger Street; each step was heavy and lethargic and arduous.

"I want coffee," he thought; "coffee, coffee, coffee." He trudged to the Junick Coffee Roastery cafe on Linden Street and took a seat inside by the window. He ordered a big German breakfast and a coffee with milk. The coffee arrived without delay. The soothing aroma hit his nose and relaxed his shoulders. "At least coffee still loves me," he thought. He took a printed newspaper from a rack on the wall and tried to read the articles on the front page but couldn't concentrate. He put it back and sat quietly in a daze sipping his coffee, staring out the window, watching the light foot traffic pass by. His breakfast arrived. He spread the butter and jam on his bread, cracked open his hard-boiled egg, and ravenously consumed it all with the sliced cheeses and deli meats. He gulped down the last drop of coffee. "I want more coffee," he thought; "I want more food." He ordered a pot of coffee and another big German breakfast. When it arrived, he ate it all,—every single bite,—in between gluttonous gulps of coffee until it was all gone. It made him feel a little less overwhelmed. He crossed his arms and leaned back in his chair. An old man with a limping dog walked past the window. "Something about people watching never gets old," he thought; "why can't I just sit here all day instead of getting swept up in the torrents of international espionage?"

He looked at his watch. It was 11:50 a.m.

"Oh, shit," he said through gritted teeth, slamming his hand on the table. His untouched glass of water tipped over, spilled into his lap, and smashed to pieces on the floor. "Oh, you clumsy fool!" he muttered to himself. He dabbed irritably at his pants with a napkin but achieved nothing. "Oh, to hell with it!"

He collected his coat, shoved cash at the waiter,—apologizing profusely,—and hurried out the door. He jogged down Linden Street, down Hegel Alley, and down Schopenhauer Street. In minutes, he entered Sanssouci Park. He sweated as he jogged down Haupt Alley: the wide main gravel pathway through the park. Finally, fatiguing, he jogged to the white marble benches surrounding the very large, round fountain pool at the base of the Vineyard Terrace retaining wall steps leading up to the decrepit Sanssouci Palace at the top of the hill: the former summer palace of Frederick II, king of Prussia. The fountain itself was turned off for winter. Hot and damp in his layers of clothing, Karsten sat on a marble bench and groaned. There were no tourists in sight. He checked his watch.

"Made it," he thought.

He peered down Haupt Alley, barely able to contain his agitation. Nobody appeared. He looked at the timber boxes,—temporarily erected around the fountain pool statues to protect them from the harsh elements of winter,—and wondered what private discussions, arguments, and confessions they had heard in times past; what secrets Frederick II had told them.

*

A man appeared in the distance on the Haupt Alley pathway. Karsten squinted: the shoulders and the stride were unmistakable. Wearing a casual coat and a beanie, the man,—not hurrying,—strode warily toward Karsten with his head down. On arrival, he reached out and shook Karsten's hand firmly.

"Good afternoon," said Michael cheerlessly, taking a seat next to him.

"Good afternoon," said Karsten, keeping a wary eye on the pathway. "You look exhausted. Why didn't you involve me sooner?"

"We made our pact a long time ago, thinking such a terrible thing would never happen again," said Michael frankly. "And now that it has, I wanted to protect you, and the others, and Theo, from getting involved. But I failed."

"It's not over yet," said Karsten.

Michael sighed.

"No, but it's a mess," he said.

"Well, I could've ignored your chalk marks," said Karsten. "But I came. Here I am."

"Thank you," said Michael graciously.

"Now tell me: What's this really about?" said Karsten intently.

"You've probably figured most of it out for yourself already," said Michael.

"How many of us did you activate?" said Karsten.

"Altogether, five out of the original seven," said Michael.

"I hope you didn't activate Esser," said Karsten with concern.

"No, I didn't activate Esser," said Michael.

"Good, he can't be trusted," said Karsten.

"And Brauer works in Washington now," said Michael.

"When did that happen?" said Karsten.

"Last year," said Michael.

"He might still be useful," said Karsten.

"No," said Michael, shaking his head. "He's been *Americanized.* He consults for them now."

"So that leaves Lehrer, Althaus, and Plank," said Karsten.

"Yeah," said Michael, nodding.

"Good, I think they're still trustworthy," said Karsten.

*

A tourist couple appeared on the pathway. Michael and Karsten waited for them to walk to the fountain pool, take photos, and walk up the retaining wall steps toward the palace.

"Hopefully they all got my signals," said Michael, watching the tourists move farther away.

"Lucky you didn't get caught," said Karsten.

"Very lucky," said Michael. "I wasn't sure I'd make it."

"You and your chalk marks," said Karsten.

"Me and my chalk marks," said Michael wearily.

A man and a woman appeared in the distance on the pathway.

"Here they come," said Karsten.

From the opposite direction, a third person appeared on the pathway and walked toward them.

"Mm-hmm," hummed Michael.

"I can't believe the pact we made as a joke thirty years ago is really happening," said Karsten, shaking his head with incredulity. "We were all just a bunch of B.N.D. recruits... fresh out of university."

"I know, it's terrifying," said Michael numbly.

The newcomers approached. Michael and Karsten stood, greeted them, shook their hands, and sat back down. The newcomers remained standing, facing them.

"Okay, Michael, what's this all about?" said Lehrer.

"Well, I'm sure you've all seen Theo's video by now, it's——" said Michael.

"Of course I've seen it," snapped Lehrer. "I don't live in a cave. But it was just a bunch of unsubstantiated claims. No facts, no evidence. What's really going on? What did you do?" he demanded.

All eyes focused on Michael.

"They abducted——" he said.

"Yes, we heard about the abduction and the threats, but that's not the point," said Lehrer sharply. "Why, Michael? Why? What did you *do* to provoke the Americans?"

"I... obtained," said Michael, choosing his words carefully, "the selector lists and operational documents from the N.S.A.'s Hemispheric Ax program."

"I'm not aware of it," said Lehrer bluntly.

"It's an American-eyes-only program," said Michael. "None of us... the B.N.D. was never supposed to know about it, but I——"

"What does it *do*?" demanded Lehrer.

Michael took a deep breath.

"They intercept and analyze the communications of every elected German politician," he said calmly. "Every federal and state politician in Germany."

"Shit," said Althaus, running a hand across her forehead. She tucked her long, silver-gray hair behind her ear. "It's run out of Passau, isn't it?"

"Yes," said Michael.

"Shit," said Althaus. "I knew that N.S.A. team was up to something fishy. I was down there last month."

"I reported it to the director, but he didn't want to talk about it," said Michael. "Chancellor Kraft knows about it too, but they don't want to upset the Americans, so they're just letting it happen." He wrung his hands together. Plank mumbled something to himself and prepared to speak but stopped himself. "They're building a blackmail database of compromising information on all our politicians," said Michael.

"It's the end of democracy," said Plank slowly.

Michael nodded.

"I was about to blow the whistle but the Americans *intervened* before I had the chance," he said.

"Mm," grumbled Lehrer.

"The public must know what's being done against them," said Michael insistently. "It's our obligation as responsible citizens."

"Indira Chandra!" said Lehrer bitingly.

"Yes, I know," said Michael. "That's how bad this is."

"If we challenge the Americans, the same fate will befall us all," said Lehrer.

"But the public must be informed," said Michael imploringly.

"But it's not the B.N.D., it's the N.S.A.," said Lehrer defensively. "They're the ones doing the surveillance."

"Not exactly," said Michael, cocking his head to one side. "There *are* B.N.D. surveillance programs that violate the law and the

B.N.D.'s mandate, and that must be shut down. *And* there is the issue of strategic N.S.A. surveillance of German politicians from within B.N.D. stations, within our own blasted borders! All with the knowledge and consent of the B.N.D. director... and the chancellor! And probably the minister as well!"

"I think, politically," said Plank soothingly, trying to calm the situation, "the chancellor just wants to stay in power for a fourth consecutive term. And the easiest way to do that is to cooperate with the Americans, without rocking the boat. With the election coming up, any major disputes with the Americans could derail his——"

"I don't *care* if his campaign gets derailed," said Michael coolly. "The N.S.A. is a planetary Stasi and we cannot——"

"Don't use that word!" snapped Lehrer.

"Stasi?" said Michael.

"*Don't* use that word," said Lehrer, waving a finger at him threateningly. "You have no right to invoke the Stasi! You know what they did to my father! Don't you even——"

"That's exactly what the N.S.A. and its partner organizations have become," said Michael decisively. "Much worse actually: the most extensive and pervasive citizen surveillance system of all time. That's what it is: a planetary Stasi network designed to increase the power of the governments,—and the individuals,—who control it. It gives them the power to suppress and control their citizens, and their opponents. We have to call it what it is. Anything else is an outrageous charade! The N.S.A. and the B.N.D. are police state surveillance services."

"Michael," said Lehrer in a condescending tone.

"We swore we would prevent the B.N.D. from turning into another Stasi," said Michael.

"We were all *drunk* when we made the pact, Michael," said Lehrer inflexibly. "It was a stupid joke!"

"But it's happening for real!" said Michael.

"I'm out!" declared Lehrer, throwing his hands up. "I'm not dying for this. I've got two kids, a pregnant wife, a dog, and a mortgage." He turned and strode hastily up the pathway, the way he had come. "I want no part in this! Keep me out of it!" he called over his shoulder. "I was never here!"

"Thank you for coming!" called Michael.

"This isn't good," said Althaus, putting her hands on her hips.

Lehrer disappeared from view.

"Shit," said Michael, massaging his forehead.

"He never intended to get involved, but he was too curious to stay away," said Plank.

Althaus raised her eyebrows.

"He'll keep quiet," said Michael. "I don't think we have to worry about him."

"Probably not," said Karsten.

"That leaves four of us," said Althaus pessimistically.

"We still have the same responsibility to act," said Karsten.

"I'm not disagreeing with that," said Althaus. "But four of us can only do so much."

"Mass surveillance is like an opiate addiction," said Plank ponderously. "Everybody knows it's wrong, but once the government is addicted and physically dependent on it, it lashes out with extremely violent withdrawal reactions whenever it gets challenged on it." He looked up at the gray sky. "We need to get the B.N.D. onto a detox program of public transparency, accountability, and oversight."

"Ah, don't all turn around at once," said Karsten, looking down the pathway, "but, Michael, I thought you said you didn't activate Esser."

"Yeah," said Michael, slowly turning his head to follow Karsten's gaze.

"Because I swear that's him on the pathway," said Karsten.

"Shit," said Althaus, without turning around to look.

Michael squinted at the person on the pathway.

"Blast!" said Michael. "Yeah, it's him. Gosh, he's aged badly."

"He must have been staking this place out," said Althaus.

"If he reports us to the director, we'll all be in handcuffs before sunset," said Plank prophetically, looking to Michael.

"We have to stop him," said Michael. "We have to talk him down."

"Is he moving?" said Althaus.

"He's doing exactly what we're doing," said Michael. "Watching."

"Well then, we're in this for real now," said Karsten.

"For democracy," said Plank unenthusiastically.

"It's the right thing to do," said Althaus.

"I'm armed," said Karsten to Michael. "You?"

"Yeah," said Michael, nodding.

"I'm not," said Althaus.

"Me neither," said Plank.

"Do you have a car nearby?" said Michael to Plank.

"Yes," said Plank.

"Okay, on the count of three, you go out another way," said Michael. "Get your car and wait by the Haupt Alley entrance on Schopenhauer Street with the engine running, clear?"

"Clear," said Plank.

"You two," said Michael to Althaus and Karsten, "you come with me to confront Esser, clear?"

"Clear," said Karsten.

"Clear," said Althaus.

"Okay, on three," said Michael. "Three, two, one."

Plank walked briskly up the pathway. Michael stood and began walking toward Esser. Karsten and Althaus walked with him. Sixty meters away, watching them with his hands in his pockets, Esser took two cautious steps backward and froze.

"Esser hates me," said Karsten quietly, trying not to move his lips. "I suspended him for illegally torturing one of the Bonn bombers during an interrogation, but I was overruled by the director. Eventually, I transferred Esser out of my division. He hasn't spoken a word to me since. Stay alert."

"Understood," said Althaus.

"The only way out is through," said Michael to himself under his breath. Karsten groaned uneasily. Suddenly, Esser turned and sprinted away like a startled animal. "Charge him in a pincer movement, I'll go straight!" said Michael, breaking into a run. "Esser!" he shouted, charging after him. "Wait!"

Althaus ran to the left of Michael. Karsten ran to the right of Michael. Ahead of them, Esser turned off the pathway and disappeared into the trees.

"Blast!" huffed Karsten.

Althaus darted around a hedge and spotted Esser. She ran wide to his left and gained ground, huffing and puffing and grunting with exertion. Esser looked over his shoulder and saw her getting closer. He grunted and ran faster. Michael lagged behind, too exhausted to keep up. Karsten lost ground fighting his way through a thick cluster of low-hanging tree branches. He tripped on an exposed tree root and tumbled to the ground, grunting and groaning. He picked himself up and continued running. Racing swiftly through the trees, Althaus edged closer and closer. Wheezing lethargically, Esser zigzagged around a hedge,—losing speed with the maneuver,—and ran in a straight line, trying to speed up. Althaus sensed her chance. She hurdled over the hedge and closed in with a burst of extra speed. She lunged forward and threw her arm out to grab him.

"Argh!" grunted Esser, dodging her arm. He stopped dead in his tracks, whipped out his gun, chambered a round, steadied his legs in a firing stance, and aimed directly at Althaus' chest. "Get back!" he barked viciously. "Get back, you filthy traitor!"

Michael slowed to a walk and approached them with his hands up, sucking in deep breaths.

"Just... take it easy," he huffed. "We——"

Bang! Bang! Two gunshots rang out from the trees. Esser crumpled to the ground,—dropping his gun,—and clutched his chest with both hands, crying out in agony. Karsten stepped out from the trees with his gun trained on Esser and paused to catch his breath. Esser moaned and quickly reached for his gun. Karsten looked to Michael for approval. Michael nodded. Esser grabbed his gun. Karsten focused and steadied his aim. Bang! He shot Esser. Bang! Karsten shot him dead. Michael squatted in place and rested his elbows on his knees, looking at the body.

"We have to get out of here without being seen," said Althaus.

XVI.

STRASBOURG, FRANCE. TWO DAYS LATER. The doorbell rang at 6:03 a.m. Pierre crawled out of bed and shuffled to the intercom in the living room, rubbing his eyes. Awakened, Theo watched him from the couch, wrapped in a blanket.

"If it's for you, I'll tell them you're not here," said Pierre.

"Sure," said Theo resignedly. "Everybody already knows I'm here."

Pierre pressed the intercom.

"Hello, who is it?" he said.

"Good morning, I'm Karsten Bender," said Karsten unhurriedly. "Theo knows who I am. Please tell him I'm here."

"Yeah, I know him," said Theo, getting up from the couch.

Pierre took his finger off the intercom and looked at him curiously.

"*How* do you know him?" said Pierre.

"He's my father's oldest friend," said Theo. "They went to university together. They've been colleagues for decades."

"But can you trust him?" said Pierre.

"Yes," said Theo, without hesitation. He pressed the intercom. "Hello, Karsten?"

"Hello, young man," said Karsten.

"Gee, am I glad to hear your voice," said Theo.

"Can you let me up, please?" said Karsten, telling more than asking.

"Oh sure, of course, come on up," said Theo, buzzing him in. "Second floor, first door on the left."

Theo unlocked and opened the apartment door and listened to Karsten's footsteps coming up the stairwell. At the first sight of him, Theo bounded out the door and hugged him.

"Hello, young man," said Karsten benevolently, taking a duffel bag off his shoulder. "You look more and more like your father every time I see you."

"Is that a good thing or a bad thing?" said Theo.

Karsten bit his lip. He walked in and motioned with his head for Theo to follow him into the bathroom. He turned on the sink taps, the shower, and the exhaust fan, and closed the door. He laid the duffel bag on the linoleum floor and cupped his hands around Theo's ear.

"There's a change of clothes in here," said Karsten. "Shoes, socks, underwear; everything. I had to guess your size, so if it's too big, I'm sorry. You need to remove all other clothes, accessories, and devices, and change into these. Any of your old stuff could be fitted with tracking devices or have tracer compounds on it," he said, cautioning. "No wristwatches or wristbands; nothing. Just the new clothes in this bag. Get changed quickly."

He put his hands on Theo's shoulders and nodded for him to consent. Theo nodded. Karsten stepped out of the bathroom, closed the door, and waited by the couch in the living room. He checked his watch and nodded with content.

*

Standing by the front door, wondering what was going on, Pierre stared in silence, sensing that now was not the time to engage in small talk. Theo emerged from the bathroom in the new clothes and handed the empty duffel bag to Karsten.

"Say goodbye," whispered Karsten to Theo.

Theo hugged Pierre, silently mouthed his thanks, and followed Karsten out the door and down the stairs. A B.M.W. with diplomatic German license plates was waiting in front of the building with the engine running. Another man was in the driver's seat. Karsten and Theo got in. The driver acknowledged that the coast was clear and took off before they had a chance to clip in their seat belts. Karsten flipped down the front passenger seat visor and adjusted it to watch the cars behind them in the visor mirror.

"Two cars back," said the driver, keeping his eyes on the road ahead.

"Mm, I see them," said Karsten. "The C.I.A.'s been keeping a close watch on you," he said to Theo.

"The D.G.S.I. paid me a visit too," said Theo.

"Oh, really," said Karsten, half distracted. "The silver Volkswagen?" he said to the driver.

"Yeah," said the driver curtly.

"Where's my father?" said Theo.

"This is not the place to discuss your father," said Karsten. The driver zipped them firmly around corners and promptly down side streets. The C.I.A. car followed them at every turn; and onto the autoroute. "I don't like this," said Karsten to the driver, watching the visor mirror. "Speed. Floor it all the way there."

The driver accelerated and weaved skillfully around the light traffic. Behind them, the C.I.A. car accelerated and kept pace.

"I can't lose them this way," said the driver.

"Just keep going, and don't slow down," said Karsten, remaining calm.

"You've blown your cover by coming to get me," said Theo.

"I know," said Karsten. "But would you have trusted anybody else?"

"Just you or my father," said Theo.

"Exactly," said Karsten. "And he'd be shot on sight."

"Thank you for doing this," said Theo.

"Of course, you're welcome," said Karsten. "But we're not welcome in Germany anymore. The chancellor's compromised, the B.N.D.'s compromised, and," he shook his head, "and we need to get off the road before the fools following us figure out I'm B.N.D. They might overreact when they do, and I don't think it'll take them long."

"Oh," said Theo, gripping the door handle more tightly.

Strasbourg airport came into view. Karsten continued to watch the visor mirror.

"I'm sorry I couldn't come get you sooner," he said. "I had to make some... arrangements."

"I'm just glad you came at all," said Theo. "But I didn't expect all this to happen. I thought my father would simply release the documents once he saw my video."

"It was a clever strategy, but it hasn't played out that way," said Karsten kindly. "Some very large cogs have been set in motion now; some very large mountains have been moved." He looked ahead at the fast-approaching airport with mounting anticipation. They exited the autoroute without indicating, sped down and around the side roads, and braked heavily at a set of security gates. The security guard recognized the license plates and waved them through. They drove in. Karsten turned around in his seat and watched the C.I.A. car slow outside the security gates, unable to follow them in. "Ah," he grinned shrewdly.

The driver zipped them onto the airport apron, drove in a bee-line past a row of parked aircraft, and pulled up behind a German air force cargo plane. The rear loading ramp was down. Karsten got out of the car, ushered Theo up the loading ramp, and waved the driver off with a casual salute. Three crew members,—a pilot, a copilot, and a flight engineer,—came out and greeted Karsten with zealous reverence. Theo was surprised.

"Why are they acting like it's an honor just to shake Karsten's hand?" he thought.

Karsten gave the instruction to depart and helped Theo into a sidewall troop seat. The four Airbus turboprop engines whined to life and filled the air with vibrations. The flight engineer closed the loading ramp. Karsten clipped himself into the troop seat next to Theo.

"Where are we going?" said Theo above the noise.

"First stop: Wunstorf Air Base," said Karsten.

"What's at Wunstorf?" said Theo.

"The cargo plane base," said Karsten.

"Why are we going there?" said Theo.

"The Americans can track us to Wunstorf,—they track all our troop movements,—but they can't monitor my activities on base," said Karsten, winking confidently.

Theo relaxed into his seat and almost smiled for the first time in days.

"I hope Davnok's okay," he said.

The confidence disappeared from Karsten's eyes.

"The Americans have lost their minds," he said sorrowfully.

"The American *government*," said Theo. "The American people are innocent. It's their government that's insane."

"Yes," said Karsten. "Same with Germany."

"People want peace, governments want war," said Theo.

Karsten closed his eyes and nodded.

XVII.

SOMEWHERE IN SOUTHERN GERMANY. FIVE DAYS LATER. Wearing a combat uniform and a bulletproof vest, Plank switched off the car's headlights and turned down an unsealed country road. Shadows of moonlight chanced through the clouds and guided his way. The road rose and fell and twisted and turned. The surrounding trees became taller and taller; he drove slower and slower; and the way ahead became darker and darker. He spotted two long vans parked to the side of the road and pulled up quietly beside them. As he got out and gently shut the door, Althaus came out of the darkness.

"I hope the kid's still alive," said Plank, fumbling for Althaus' arm in the shadows and shaking her hand.

"We think he is," said Althaus evenly.

"Can you trust your informant?" said Plank.

"I think so," said Althaus.

Plank exhaled a long breath, puffing out his cheeks.

"I still can't believe you got the location," he said. "I can't shake the feeling it's a setup."

"My gut says not," said Althaus.

"My gut wants to vomit," said Plank woefully.

"I used an independent source to verify it's C.I.A.," said Althaus. "We believe they're holding someone."

"How reliable is your source?" said Plank.

"Very reliable," said Althaus.

"Okay," said Plank. "Okay then."

He looked up at the moon hiding behind the clouds.

"Here," said Althaus. She led him into one of the vans and shut the door. It was a mobile surveillance van. Inside, a communications officer nodded politely to Plank and turned back to the panels and screens of information and video feeds. "The house is just over the hill," said Althaus, taking a seat on a small bench behind the communications officer. "The team is in position, ready to move in." She reached forward and held down a button on the control panel. "Rex, this is Lighthouse. You may proceed with the operation at will," she said, looking keenly at Rex's night vision video feed.

"Yes, ma'am," reported Rex, the team leader.

The counterterrorism team crept over the hill and took up positions around the small country house. At the rear, two soldiers lay on their stomachs,—hidden among the trees,—and covered the back door. At the front, the other soldiers spread out and edged cautiously toward the front door.

"My goodness, I hope the kid's alive," said Plank.

He put a hand over his mouth, held his breath, and watched the screens intently. Rex and his team breached the front door with a loud crack,—as the doorframe splintered around the lock,—and quickly and quietly teemed inside carrying ballistic entry shields. There was a warning shout from an occupant in a back room and semi-automatic gunshots rang out, bursting the lull of the night. The team returned fire with a volley of bullets that ripped through the walls. Back and forth, bullets flew. Within twenty seconds, it was all over; and the house fell silent. A shard of broken glass fell and shattered in the gloom. Althaus stared at the screens with bated breath. The team worked their way methodically through each room to the back of the house, where they found the bodies of two shooters, and down to the basement, where they found a hostage.

"All clear," reported Rex from the basement. "No injuries sustained; two hostiles dead; one male hostage... alive."

"Where's the third hostile?" said Plank with concern. "There should be a three-person team guarding a hostage."

"Is it him?" said Althaus with an edge in her voice.

With a teammate standing next to him, Rex kneeled next to the bound and gagged hostage and put a hand on his shoulder.

"Can you hear me?" said Rex loudly.

"Mm," groaned the hostage feebly.

"We're not here to hurt you, we're here to help you," said Rex.

He rolled the hostage onto his side and removed the gag and blindfold. The hostage inhaled shallow breaths and rested his head on the floor. His face was bruised and his lip was swollen. He blinked and closed his eyes.

"Is it him, Rex?" said Althaus intently.

Rex leaned lower.

"Can you open your eyes for me, please?" he said, squeezing the hostage's shoulder. The hostage opened his eyes. "Looks like him," reported Rex. "Can you tell me your name, please?" he said, shaking the hostage's shoulder gently.

"Davnok," said Davnok in a whisper.

"It's him," reported Rex. "He needs medical attention."

"Get him out of there," said Althaus approvingly.

With a sad, wise grin, she patted Plank on the back. Plank shook his head and slumped against the wall of the van with an uneasy sigh. The communications officer turned in his chair and smiled.

XVIII.

FOUR DAYS LATER. Theo stood on the edge of a cracked and disused runway in the shade of a rusted, domed hangar, surrounded by the undulating hills of Ecuador. He crossed his arms, uncrossed his arms, inhaled deeply, exhaled loudly, rested his hands on his hips, paced back and forth, and put his hands on his head.

"Come on," he grumbled impatiently.

"Just be grateful he's alive," called Karsten from an old deck chair next to their car in the hangar. "And come back in under the roof please. Don't make it too easy for satellites and drones to spot you out in the open."

Theo did as he was asked and sat down, crossing his legs. He stared out at the surrounding hilltops and hummed impatiently. The buzz of a single-engine aircraft became audible. It buzzed closer and louder. Theo stood up and looked about, listening eagerly. An old Cessna with white and yellow stripes appeared, floating in a sky of blue. It descended breezily, taking its time, and touched down with a bump. It whirred its way along the runway and taxied into the hangar, coming to a stop near the car. The engine powered down. The pilot nodded to Plank in the copilot's seat. Plank opened the door and helped Davnok out. Davnok's face was bruised and his arm was in a sling. Theo bounded to him and hugged him.

"Ow," winced Davnok. "Careful, they broke my arm."

"Ooh, sorry," said Theo, looking up into his eyes, smiling.

"How are——" said Davnok.

Theo kissed him quickly.

"Been dying to do that," said Theo, grinning.

Davnok chuckled.

"Mm, my lip stings, but that felt good," he said.

"You earned a kiss," said Theo.

Davnok closed his eyes.

"No words," he said, shaking his head. "No words." He took hold of Theo's bicep with his good hand. "I saw your video. You——"

"It was the only way to defuse the situation," said Theo rapidly. "They would've killed you had I done what they said."

Davnok stroked Theo's neck with his thumb.

"I was mad when they showed me your video," he said. "But I've had time to mull it over and," he faltered, "and I guess it was the best option in a bad situation. You are a bit of a political mastermind."

"You know I hate politics," said Theo disdainfully.

"But you are good at it," said Davnok. "Anyway, the way they... treated me, I don't think they intended to let me go. But," he smiled, "maybe we should hang out a bit more before you start calling me your boyfriend."

Theo grinned sheepishly.

"Of course," he said. "I guess my emotions got the better of me in the moment. I didn't realize I'd said that until——"

Davnok nodded that he understood.

"It's okay," he said. "Now I know you have the balls to admit you like me."

Theo's grin widened into a full smile.

"I'm so glad you're okay," he said.

"Come on, boys," called Karsten as he started the car. "The journey's not over yet."

XIX.

SUCRE, BOLIVIA. TWO DAYS LATER.

"This," said Karsten, as he ushered Davnok and Theo into the third-floor apartment, "is our safe house. This," he closed the door and flattened his hand against it, "is reinforced with steel: it's bullet-resistant, not bulletproof. None of the neighboring buildings has a line of sight into the apartment, and there is enough food and supplies stockpiled in the cupboards and the freezer in the laundry to last us six months. There's no need to leave the apartment." He gave them a tour of the rooms, pointed out the noteworthy features, and explained the rules of staying hidden and safe in the safe house. "And you must,—absolutely,—avoid communicating with anybody in the outside world, under any circumstances." He nodded and hummed with satisfaction. "And now that I've explained the rules, I have to disappear briefly."

"But we just got here," said Theo, protesting.

"I have to make a live drop to get a message to your father; to tell him you're safe," said Karsten. "I have a Resistance contact here. I'll be back tomorrow morning."

"Thank you for everything," said Davnok.

"My pleasure," said Karsten.

"Be careful," said Theo.

"Of course," said Karsten. He hugged Theo and shook Davnok's good hand. "Now, be safe... stay safe. And make sure you bolt the door behind me."

He winked conspiratorially and let himself out of the apartment. Theo bolted the door, put his hands around Davnok's waist, and rubbed his nose gently against Davnok's nose.

"So here we are," said Davnok. "Here we are. Bolivia. A safe house. Did you ever imagine?"

"Not in a million years," said Theo, shaking his head.

Davnok put his hand gently on Theo's neck.

"Shall I make us some coffee to settle in?" said Davnok.

Theo chuckled.

"So-o-o predictable," he said. "Yes, please."

XX.

LA PAZ, BOLIVIA. THREE DAYS LATER. Sullen and exhausted, Michael sat in a leather chair in Tarik's room at the artfully designed Atix Hotel. He was freshly shaven, his hair was neatly brushed, and he wore a pressed shirt. But he couldn't hide the dark rings under his eyes. Tarik and Henry fussed around him, buzzing with enthusiasm, adjusting the light boxes and the video camera. Tarik sat down in a chair facing Michael.

"Stories like this are the reason I became a journalist," said Tarik. "Are you ready?"

"As I'll ever be," said Michael, exhaling.

"Ready?" said Tarik to Henry, as he flipped through his handwritten notes.

Henry stood behind the camera.

"Ready," he said.

Michael pulled a small piece of paper out of his pocket, held it at his side, and reread it. It was a handwritten, hand-signed message from Karsten, confirming that Theo and Davnok had been safely stowed away.

"The only way out is through," thought Michael; "the only way out is through."

He slipped the note back into his pocket and stretched his neck.

"Okay, let's begin," said Tarik.

Michael straightened up.

"And... I'm recording," said Henry.

Tarik looked at the camera.

"I'm Tarik al-Amin with the *Intercept*," he said. "Here with me is Michael Mittendorf: a B.N.D. intelligence officer turned whistleblower. Michael, could you introduce yourself and tell us a bit about your career at the B.N.D.?"

"Certainly," said Michael. "My name's Michael Mittendorf, I was born in Bielefeld, I'm fifty-seven, and I began my career at the B.N.D. in my early twenties. Since that time, I've been an intelligence officer, an intercept analyst, a senior strategic analyst, an infrastructure advisor, and director of intelligence analysis."

He stroked his jaw with resignation.

"And can you tell us about the N.S.A.'s Hemispheric Ax program?" said Tarik.

"Yes, I can," said Michael, nodding. "The N.S.A. intercepts and analyzes the communications of all elected German politicians; all federal- and state-level politicians. The program is run out of the B.N.D. station at Passau with the full knowledge of the B.N.D. director, and Chancellor Kraft. They are complicit. I have the selector lists and other operational documents to prove it. The intelligence products produced by Hemispheric Ax are used by the United States government to gain informational advantages over Germany for political, intelligence, military, and economic purposes. Basically, it's about information supremacy. The United States government can now blackmail German politicians into doing whatever it wants; overtly and covertly; directly and indirectly. All our politicians are compromised now,—all of them,—Chancellor Kraft first and foremost."

"Those are very serious allegations," said Tarik.

"I have the documentation to prove it," said Michael firmly.

"But which is it?" said Tarik. "Is the N.S.A. or the B.N.D. Responsible?"

"Both," said Michael. "There are two separate issues here." He leaned forward. "Firstly, there's the issue of N.S.A. surveillance of German politicians. This is being conducted in our own territory. A complete violation of German sovereignty; and a complete abdication of responsibility by Chancellor Kraft and the B.N.D. director. It's treason to——"

"Treason?" said Tarik, his eyes widening.

"Yes, treason," said Michael resolutely. "We have to be honest about what's happening. There's no time for games," he said, shaking his head. "Secondly, there's the issue of illegal B.N.D. surveillance programs,—operated by the B.N.D. using American technology,—that violate the B.N.D.'s mandate and the law. German mass surveillance programs are part of a larger, planetary trend toward building mass surveillance systems that monitor billions of innocent citizens, every minute of every day. It's absolute madness! We must shut down all mass surveillance programs. We must delete all mass surveillance data."

"Are you saying the B.N.D.'s part of a global surveillance system?" said Tarik.

"Yes," said Michael. "The N.S.A.,—the United States,—is the epicenter of it. The Five Eyes alliance countries,—Australia, Canada, New Zealand, the United Kingdom, and the United States,—are the principal architects and operators of the system; and other countries, such as Germany, have become part of the system. The integration process has been escalating for many years. The public does not know the extent of it."

"What about the Edward Snowden revelations?" said Tarik. "Didn't they raise public awareness?"

"The Snowden revelations did increase public awareness," said Michael. "But mass surveillance activities have escalated radically since then. What we're seeing now is only the beginning of citizen suppression. That's what comes next. History is very clear on this point. What's happening around the planet is the conversion of democratic states into police states where elections become meaningless because our governments have accumulated too much power. They do the opposite of what their publics want them to do. And the abilities of publics to know what their governments are doing,—and to oppose them,—are sabotaged. And let me be crystal clear: it is not a conspiracy," he said, shaking his head slowly. "It is thousands of bad people in positions of authority,—all around the planet,—acting selfishly to increase their personal wealth and power. What we're seeing,—on a planetary scale,—is the aggregate consequences of this bad behavior. It's destroying our democratic checks and balances against abuses of power."

"Is the escalation the reason you're blowing the whistle?" said Tarik.

"I want my son to live in a free and democratic German republic," said Michael. "I'm doing this for him, for his future."

"When did you decide to blow the whistle?" said Tarik.

"I don't know exactly," said Michael. "Perhaps about two years ago. I fought against mass surveillance programs for years internally. But my superiors never listened. They said I was the problem. I realized I had to act. I realized the government was becoming a police state. And I must say: I'm ashamed of what the B.N.D. has become. It's an abomination! A desecration of my life's work to protect Germany. Espionage is a function of war; and spying on all citizens makes us all enemies of state."

"Some might say calling the German government a police state is going too far," said Tarik.

"The public can seek out verifiable facts and consider them for themselves," said Michael calmly. "They should ignore the government propaganda, the spin, and the lies, and look at the facts. Germany is almost completely deferential to the whims of the self-destructive United States government. Our country is occupied by the United States military. Ramstein Air Base is just one example. For those who don't know, Ramstein is a large American military base in Germany, occupied by thousands of United States military personnel. It is used as a launching pad for American wars in the Middle East. This makes Germany a willing participant in American government terrorism. And it's unacceptable. We must shut down all American military bases in Germany. We must expel all American military personnel from Germany. We must shut down all N.S.A. operations in Germany. And we must expel all N.S.A. personnel from Germany. Because, as things stand, we're a United States military colony."

"That's a bold statement, Michael," said Tarik.

"It's the plain truth," said Michael. "We are supposed be an independent democracy; a democracy for peace, not war. Liberty should matter to us. Privacy should matter to us."

"How do you mean?" said Tarik.

"Most people are not criminals," said Michael. "We all need privacy to think, to experiment, to make mistakes, to learn, to hope... to dream. Mass surveillance kills privacy and liberty. That's one thing. And if we kill privacy and liberty, then we kill creativity and freedom of expression and meaningful public opposition to government. Because the government will enact laws to legalize its mass surveillance activities and data collection. It will enact laws to suppress freedom of expression, public opposition, and public protests. And it will transform into a police state. This has already happened in Australia. And that should be a warning sign for us all: if you don't fight to keep your democracy, it will be taken from you while you sleep." He glared at the camera. "Once a government has mass surveillance capabilities and data, it will use them to consolidate, centralize, and increase its power over the public, in any way it can. Effectively, what the politicians are saying now is that *they* can have secrets, but *we* the public cannot: that is the opposite of democracy. Mass surveillance turns us all into criminals; the democratic presumption of innocence has been turned upside down. Now we're all presumed guilty until proven innocent." He shifted in his chair. "Justice is a fundamental pillar of democracy, and mass surveillance cracks that pillar at its foundation. And when a pillar of democracy is broken, good citizens have a moral obligation to stand up and fix it."

"That's a big topic to cover in this time-limited format," said Tarik, looking at his notepad. "Can you speak about the connection between mass surveillance and terrorism?"

"These two issues are frequently conflated," said Michael, rubbing his eye. "By the government, for political purposes, and by the media, who fail to appreciate the difference, and who simply copy and paste the words of the politicians. Politicians use reporters as talking parrots, feeding them propaganda seeds. And Chancellor Kraft continues to beat the drums of national security and terrorism to instill fear in the public. He uses fear... he preaches fear and hatred to get reelected by presenting himself as the solution to fear,—just like President Hawk did in her campaign,—and he continues to demand ever-increasing levels of security: harsher laws, harsher policies. The chancellor claims that more security measures are needed to combat terrorism; to keep people safe. But that's a lie," he said, displaying his palms. "Most B.N.D. surveillance is *not* related to terrorism at all. In fact, Andrea Vosshoff, the federal commissioner for data protection and freedom of information, publicly confirmed that less than ten percent of B.N.D. surveillance is related to terrorism. In her report, she blasted the B.N.D. for collecting personal data without any legal basis, and for continuing to use it systematically. I'm paraphrasing what she said, but the facts are clear: most B.N.D. surveillance is completely unnecessary surveillance of innocent citizens."

"Indeed," said Tarik. "And on that topic, at the *Intercept* we published a report that analyzed terrorist attacks in the West. We found that most of the suspects were already known to authorities,— already considered to be potential threats,—and were already listed on some form of watch list. But most weren't properly followed up by traditional law enforcement under traditional law enforcement laws and procedures. And mass surveillance completely failed to prevent the attacks."

"Exactly," said Michael. "And there's no such thing as a perfectly safe society. It's a myth: no politician can deliver that. Even when criminals are properly followed up with traditional law enforcement, it's impossible to know their futures."

"Indeed——" said Tarik.

"I should add that traditional, targeted surveillance of known criminals, and traditional law enforcement methods and laws, are far superior at dealing with terrorism than mass surveillance," said Michael. "But traditional law enforcement isn't being properly used or resourced. All the time and money is being wasted on mass surveillance. But mass surveillance is a much bigger threat to democracy than it is beneficial to our security."

"What's the alternative then?" said Tarik.

"The problem is the supremacy fallacy," said Michael. "That's something we need to expose and discuss," he said sincerely. "Rich and powerful countries falsely presume themselves to be superior to weaker and poorer countries. And so, the powerful grant themselves the right to dominate and subjugate the weak and poor by force. That's why, when an attack occurs in a Western country, our governments howl solidarity with each other, and proclaim it to be an attack on Western values and culture and our way of life. That's complete nonsense. They just don't want to acknowledge the fact that Western governments are the original terrorist organizations in this chapter of history. The United States government,—and its surrogate states,—are the ones who invaded and occupied Afghanistan and Iraq, for example. This is a simple truth that people don't want to talk about: our governments are the invaders. The attacks in Western countries are retaliations for these invasions and occupations: they are retaliations for the slaughter and displacement of millions of innocent people. Retaliatory attacks are the only means these people have left to fight with. And the attacks will not stop until the United States empire withdraws from occupied territories, and allows them to govern themselves, on their own terms, without interference. They must be treated with dignity and respect."

"But the Americans will never withdraw," said Tarik, shaking his head in disbelief.

"And *that* is the cause of all this planetary suffering," said Michael. "All this death, all this destruction, all this fear, all this hatred. I'll say it again: the only way to stop retaliatory attacks is for invading foreign states to completely withdraw from occupied territories in the Middle East, and elsewhere."

"Well that——" said Tarik.

"The solutions to many of our planetary problems are

scandalously simple, if you actually bother to look for them," said Michael.

Tarik took a breath and flipped through his notepad.

"Are there other discontented people like you at the B.N.D.?" he said.

"Yes, there are many others," said Michael, wiping his brow. "At the B.N.D., in the military, in the civil service, all over the country. And I call on every responsible German to stand up and resist the establishment of another police state in Germany!" He looked directly at the camera. "We must resist this treasonous government! We must protect our democratic republic! And we must do it now!"

"What you're describing sounds like an anti-American resistance," said Tarik cautiously.

"No," said Michael gravely. "It's a genuine, democratic German resistance to stop the establishment of a police state in Germany. If we don't resist,—immediately,—then it will take a revolution to stop it."

XXI.

SUCRE, BOLIVIA. Karsten bolted through the nighttime shadows of the Plaza 25 de Mayo as fast as his long legs could carry him. He stretched them out with each stride and his soles slapped the pavement. He sprinted around the monument to Antonio José de Sucre. Bang! A lone gunshot rang out from close behind. He exited the plaza, crossed the street,—dodging traffic,—and turned down España Street, running full pelt.

"Where are you?" he huffed urgently.

"White car, facing away from the plaza," said a young man in his earpiece.

Karsten scanned the street ahead.

"Where?" he huffed.

"White car," said the young man. "I'm waving out the window, parked to the side."

"I see you," said Karsten, running through the darkness. "Start the engine!"

"What's going on?" said the young man, as he started the car.

"I'm being shot at!" shouted Karsten. "Just do it!" Bang! A bullet struck the wall barely meters from him; the gunshot echoed and bounced between the surrounding buildings. Bang! Another miss. "Urgh!" he grunted, urging himself onward. "Start moving!" he huffed. He fired two rounds randomly in his wake to ward off his attackers. Ahead of him, the white car began to move away. Karsten caught up, wrenched the passenger side door open, and threw himself in headfirst. "Evade!" he shouted. Remaining calm under pressure, the young man floored the accelerator. Bang! Bang! Bang! The rear window shattered and the young man slumped over the steering wheel. "Shit!" seethed Karsten. He fired two rounds out the rear window,—buying himself precious seconds,—hauled the young man, moaning in agony, half way out of the driver's seat, climbed over him, and shoved his leg awkwardly at the accelerator pedal. Bang! Bang! Bang! Bullets hit the car in quick succession. Vroom! Karsten thundered away, swerving from side to side to make the car a more difficult target to hit. He veered around the nearest corner at speed. "Blasted Americans!" he roared violently.

XXII.

Theo came out of the bedroom in his boxers and joined Davnok on the couch. Davnok put his good arm around Theo and stroked his hairy chest.

"Can you turn the volume up?" said Theo.

The view on the television screen shifted to Minister Kaiser, standing in a corridor of the parliamentary Reichstag Building in Berlin, surrounded by journalists waving microphones in his face, demanding answers.

"Minister, Minister Kaiser——"

"Minister, can you comment——"

"Minister, as the minister responsible for the B.N.D., can you——"

"Minister, Minister, the Mittendorf revelations——"

The minister wore a condescending expression on his permanently frowning face.

"I have spoken with Chancellor Kraft," he said, "regarding the treacherous intelligence leaks by Michael Mittendorf: a traitor to our country. He will be prosecuted to the full extent of the law——"

"They've lost their minds!" shouted Theo.

"Mm," grumbled Davnok.

"I can't believe he——" said Theo.

"Listen, listen, listen," said Davnok, his eyes riveted to the screen.

"... was a treacherous violation of his duty as a B.N.D. officer," said the minister. "Mittendorf's leaks have damaged our national security and damaged our diplomatic relationship with our United States ally who cooperate with us on——"

"The United States who you serve like slaves!" shouted Theo. "You sellout!"

"... cooperation on intelligence matters," said the minister with his nose in the air, "is essential to ensure the safety of German citizens in this era of global terrorism."

"Minister," said a journalist, "the Mittendorf revelations, the documents... they show clearly that the communications of German politicians,—all of you, Minister,—are being systematically intercepted by the N.S.A. from the B.N.D. station at Passau."

"No, no, no," said the minister, shaking his head, "those are the accusations of a disgruntled former employee of the B.N.D.; a narcissistic, antisocial deviant who just wants to be famous; a damaging leaker and a traitor who has put German lives at risk."

"Sir, are you denying——" said the journalist.

"There's nothing to deny," snapped the minister.

"Sir," said another journalist, raising his voice, "can you confirm the rumors that there are other B.N.D. insiders helping Mittendorf? Is there is a new resistance in——"

"Absolutely not," scoffed the minister, as though he were reprimanding a child. "No, no, no. Don't be so foolish! No wonder the public doesn't trust the media anymore. No, this is an isolated incident. There is no resistance. That's a preposterous suggestion. There are no rogue intelligence officers inside the B.N.D. That's fake news and you should be ashamed!" he cried, pointing his finger.

The journalists broke into a flurry of overlapping questions.

"Minister, Mittendorf revealed that——"

"Minister, according to our constitution——"

"Ahem," the minister cleared his throat, "our national security is our highest priority. We must ensure that the damage these leaks have caused is contained. Our intelligence capabilities are essential to combating terrorism——"

"Unbelievable!" said Davnok with frustration. "He's regurgitating pro-war propaganda like a sock puppet."

"He's going in totally the wrong direction," said Theo. "Hard and fast to the extreme right. Surveillance above all else. Police state security above all else. It's all so wrong!"

The journalists clamored for more answers; their calls grew louder and louder; their agitation swelled into a frenzy of barely professional rage.

"He's doubling down," said Davnok under his breath.

"He's linking it all to terrorism," said Theo angrily, massaging his temples. "That's not what this is about! It's not about terrorism! It's about N.S.A. surveillance of German politicians!" he shouted at the screen. "It's about the B.N.D.'s treason!"

"It's done," said Davnok quietly.

"What?" said Theo.

"It's over,—it's done,—it can't be stopped," said Davnok helplessly. "Look, look, look," he said, pointing at the screen.

The minister waved down the journalists and adjusted his jacket.

"Germany is a nation of laws," he said. "Michael Mittendorf will be charged for his crimes according to the law." The journalists erupted but the minister continued to speak over them. "He will face the consequences of his actions," said the minister. "He could have raised his concerns through internal channels instead of choosing to leak national security secrets to the media——"

"He did raise them!" shouted Theo.

"... damaging our national security," said the minister. "Damaging our intelligence capabilities. Damaging our important diplomatic relationship with the United States: our key ally in the global war on terror."

"You monstrous, useless, lying sack of shit!" shouted Theo.

"Minister, Minister Kaiser!" called a journalist. "How can you justify punishing a whistleblower like this?"

"Mittendorf did his duty as a German citizen!" called another journalist. "He did his civic duty to——"

"No!" exclaimed the minister irritably. "I will *not* entertain this notion! Michael Mittendorf is not a whistleblower. He is a traitor and a leaker!"

"But Minister, Minister!" shouted an offscreen journalist.

"That is all I have to say on the matter," declared the minister.

He turned away, like a general dismissing his inferiors, and strode back into the depths of parliamentary power where journalists,—and the public,—are not allowed to tread. The news host appeared and began listing the minister's key statements. Theo turned the volume down and threw his arms up.

"What in the world's going on?" he said despairingly. "The world is upside down. Germany is supposed to be a democracy, not a police state. Not an American puppet state."

"It's messed up," said Davnok, rubbing his face.

"I hope Bolivia grants him asylum," said Theo. "Because German democracy is dead."

Davnok closed his eyes.

"I think your father knew," he said, hesitating, "he must have known that he'd end up in prison if he stayed in Germany. Whistleblowers don't get heralded, they get imprisoned,—or assassinated,—if they embarrass the government too much; like Indira Chandra. History is saturated with the blood of murdered messengers."

"But this is Germany we're talking about!" said Theo hotly. "Not Iraq, not Afghanistan, not Libya, not Palestine, not Yemen! It's as if we're just another poor country for the United States to invade and conquer! They've taken over Germany without firing a single shot!"

Davnok ran a hand down his face.

"They don't have to," he said flatly. "They dropped all the bombs they needed to up to 1945. They've occupied Germany ever since. We're all part of the empire now. And if Germany is an occupied military colony, like your father says, then Australia is a tributary military colony."

"Australia?" said Theo.

"Yeah," said Davnok seriously. "The Australian government gives our military to the United States government to use however it wants. Australia invaded Iraq with the Americans, which made Australia less safe. And Australia continues to occupy Iraq with the Americans, which continues to make Australia less safe. It's crazy! Former U.N. secretary-general, Kofi Annan, himself said the invasion was illegal. The Australian government has no right to be in Iraq. But the politicians don't care. Australian prime ministers are stupid American empire sock puppets; just like German chancellors and British prime ministers," he said with disappointment.

"Gee, tell me what you really think," said Theo sardonically.

Davnok stretched his back.

"I think Switzerland is one of the only countries in the world with a responsive, functioning democratic system," he said seriously. "And it's far from perfect."

Theo grumbled.

"And now my father is a fugitive in exile," he said.

"At least he's still alive, all things considered," said Davnok. "He did what he did for you, you know."

"But this is not how things are supposed to work!" said Theo sharply. "Not in Germany. Germany is supposed to be better than this! How did we let this happen?"

Davnok shrugged.

"I'm worried about Karsten," he said.

"I don't even want to think about that," said Theo.

"He was supposed to be back days ago," said Davnok.

"I know," said Theo despondently. "But what in the universe can we do about it?"

"I hope they haven't found him," said Davnok.

"I don't even want to imagine that," said Theo, shaking his head. "I can't bear the thought."

"We're powerless," said Davnok.

"I really hoped my father would say something about his asylum status in his interview," said Theo.

"I hope *I'm* not forced to apply for asylum," said Davnok.

Theo raised his eyebrows.

"You?" he said. "The situation in Australia can't be *that* serious."

"Yeah, it is," said Davnok earnestly. "The Australian government will hate me for being associated with your father, and with you. They abandoned Julian Assange when he published Chelsea Manning's information that proved government wrongdoing. They refused to help him. He had to apply to Ecuador for asylum. The Australian government could cancel my passport and disown me too. Depends on how politicized my involvement gets."

Theo cackled morbidly and quickly covered his mouth.

"Ah, shit," he said, running a hand through his hair. "I just keep getting sucked back into politics, no matter how hard I try to get out."

"You can trust the Australian government to do the wrong thing," said Davnok regrettably. "Both major parties are shredding the remains of Australian democracy. The surveillance infrastructure is in place. Mandatory citizen surveillance slash data retention laws are in effect. Anti-labor union, anti-association, and anti-protest laws are in effect. It's completely illegal for anybody,—even journalists,—to publicly disclose official government secrets without official permission, under any circumstances. Adults,—and minors,—can be detained for weeks without being charged with a crime. Australia has no civil rights charter," he said, shaking his head. "And the executive branch of government violates international human rights law; threatens, intimidates, and raids opposition groups; ignores the public will and the public good; and worst of all, overrides the parliament and the judiciary, and abuses its power. Australia *is* a police state," he said simply.

Theo stared at him in astonishment.

XXIII.

LA PAZ, BOLIVIA. With a photography camera hanging around her neck, a floppy summer hat sitting on her head, and casual sunglasses partially hiding her face, Vanessa watched Henry,—from a distance,—as he bought pastries at a small bakery and emerged carrying paper bags. She followed him through the lazy afternoon streets, her stomach fluttering with excitement. She closed in on him as he entered the lobby of the Atix Hotel; and moseyed up behind him as he waited for the elevator. He sniffed his bags of pastries in hungry anticipation. The elevator doors chimed open and he walked in,—oblivious to Vanessa,—who followed him in. She watched him press the button for the fourth floor, then pressed it twice herself, as if she were in a hurry to get back to her room. She kept her head down. The elevator whooshed upward. Vanessa fiddled with the settings on her camera and scrolled through the photos she had taken of her food earlier that day. The elevator doors chimed open at the fourth floor. Henry stretched out his arm and held the doors open for her, but she kept her head down, pretended not to notice, and fiddled with her camera settings. Henry opened his mouth, about to say something, but decided to let it go and walked out. Vanessa counted to three, then followed him down the corridor. Henry swiped open his hotel room door and stepped inside. Vanessa caught up and tried to casually peer in after him, but the door thudded shut before she could get a proper look.

Without stopping, she walked to the end of the corridor, doubled back, and returned to the lobby. She took a seat in a plush chair and gently rested her daypack between her feet.

"Are the others with him?" said Simons, sitting in the chair next to her.

"I don't know, I couldn't see," said Vanessa, not looking at him. "But we'll know soon enough."

"Okay," said Simons.

"Book a room on the fourth floor, as close to the elevator as possible, please," said Vanessa, adjusting her summer hat.

"I'm on it," said Simons.

"Thank you," said Vanessa. "Then meet me back at the car when you're done."

"Will do," said Simons quietly.

Vanessa got up and walked out of the hotel. She crossed the street, stood in the shade of an opposing building, and let her eyes wander up the floors of the hotel.

"Ready or not," she thought, "here I come."

She called Clara's number, held her device to her ear, and gave her security code to Clara's assistant.

"What is it?" said Clara, her voice cutting through clearly from Berlin as if there were no distance between them.

"I've located and sighted Henry at the hotel," said Vanessa evenly.

"Yes-s-s!" hissed Clara. "Progress-s-s!"

"I know which room he's in," said Vanessa. "We're setting up surveillance now."

"We'll soon see if your hunch is correct," said Clara.

"We will, one way or another," said Vanessa.

"Good," said Clara. "Now listen up. A lot has been happening behind the scenes. There's been a change of plan."

XXIV.

C.N.N. NEWS ALERT: "... new reporting has just broken on this story," said Grace the C.N.N. news host. "We're crossing live to *Washington Post* reporter, Noah Hopkins, in La Paz, Bolivia, to tell us more about this breaking news. Noah, what's the situation there in La Paz?"

"Thank you, Grace," said Noah. "Yes, that's right, I'm here on location in La Paz, Bolivia. Behind me you can see the upscale Atix Hotel where the German terrorist leader, Michael Mittendorf, recorded his now infamous interview with journalists from the controversial news site, the *Intercept*. It was from here that he released his trove of secret N.S.A. documents from the Hemispheric Ax program. My sources at the State Department have confirmed that Mittendorf's terror group,—known as the Anti-American Resistance,—was added to the State Department's Foreign Terrorist Organizations list just hours ago," he said boastfully. "And, Grace, as detailed in my exclusive *Washington Post* report, my sources at the White House and the C.I.A. have confirmed that the terrorist leader, Michael Mittendorf, was killed in a U.S. special forces raid at this hotel," he said, pointing to the hotel in the background, "in the early hours of this morning. The shattered glass you can see on the sidewalk behind me is from Mittendorf's hotel room. Local residents here describe hearing a loud bang followed by gunfire at around 4:10 a.m. this morning, local time. This is where the terrorist leader was hiding from U.S. authorities. My sources have also confirmed that a second man,—Mittendorf's terrorist lieutenant,—is believed to be on the run, somewhere in South America. As detailed exclusively in my *Washington Post* report, his name is Karsten Bender. That's all we know about the terrorist lieutenant so far. This is Noah Hopkins for the *Washington Post*, reporting live from La Paz, Bolivia. Back to you in the studio, Grace."

"Thank you, Noah, for that report," said Grace. "And we'll be right back to bring you live coverage of more breaking news on this story as it develops, right here on C.N.N...."

XXV.

SUCRE, BOLIVIA. Standing in the middle of the living room, Theo stared at the television screen in shock.

"They just did it!" he said with fire in his eyes. "They just called my father a terrorist and assassinated him. Just like that!"

Davnok looked back and forth between Theo and the screen with dismay.

"I... I'm so sorry," he said, opening his arms.

"No!" said Theo, shaking his head vigorously, throwing himself onto the couch.

"I'm so sorry," said Davnok. "I wish there was something I could do." He pinched the top of his nose with his fingers. "Who knows? Maybe we're next. At least it'll be over quickly. And then we won't have to worry about it, once we're dead."

Theo trembled furiously and thumped the couch with his fists.

"Damn it!" he shouted. "Damn it! Damn it! Blasted Americans!"

"American *government*," said Davnok reflexively.

Theo glared at him.

"Yes, *I know*," said Theo angrily. "The government, not the people. We've been over this," he huffed. "I don't think they'll kill us." He took a deep breath. "I don't think——"

"How can you know that?" said Davnok tensely. "The American government is completely insane. How can you know they won't kill us next?"

"Because they haven't added us to the terrorist list," said Theo. "They're making an example of him, not us."

"Indira Chandra wasn't on the terrorist list either, but they blew her head off in broad daylight," said Davnok. "How can you be so sure some C.I.A. nutcase won't give the order to murder us too? There's no telling what——"

"Look, I can't," said Theo, shaking his head. "You know I can't. I just think it's unlikely." He drew his legs to his chest, wrapped his arms around them, and rested his chin on his knees. "Madness is unpredictable," he mumbled bitterly. "But they haven't found us yet. Let's just hope it stays that way."

XXVI.

After a sleepless night, Theo dozed uneasily in the bedroom with the curtains drawn, blocking out the overcast afternoon light. The bedroom door was ajar. Davnok sat at the kitchen table scribbling notes into a graph-ruled notebook, sipping a cup of coffee. The radio murmured quietly.

"I have to do something," thought Davnok; "I have to find a way to counterbalance this madness."

He turned on the burner laptop that Karsten had left with them and connected to the internet using the neighbor's network. He downloaded a copy of the Charter of the United Nations and disconnected the laptop. He read the Charter from beginning to end, pausing to make notes and highlight key articles, sipping his coffee.

*

As dusk fell upon the safe house, the kitchen light came on and Davnok looked up to see Theo leaning in the kitchen doorway. His face was pale and somber, and there were dark rings under his eyes.

"What are you doing sitting in the dark?" said Theo.

"Oh, I've been thinking," said Davnok.

Theo leaned over Davnok's shoulders and hugged him around the chest.

"What dangerous thinking have you been doing?" said Theo.

"The United States empire is destroying human civilization," said Davnok. "We need to stop it and de-escalate the aggression."

"Nothing like a bit of world domination to get you through the day," said Theo dryly, stretching his arms behind his head.

"Planetary peace, not planetary domination," said Davnok. "Well, perfect planetary peace is impossible; too Utopian. But more peaceful and sustainable international relations, yeah, that's certainly possible."

"Elaborate?" said Theo, resting his hands on Davnok's shoulders.

"The United States and its colonies use terror and force to dominate the planet," said Davnok. "Wildly unregulated neoliberal capitalism has become the world's dominant political religion: the mindless pursuit of wealth and power, and the obliteration of anything that gets in its way, including democracy. It creates capitalist dictatorships. Its objective is winning at any cost in the short term, consequences be damned. It's morally bankrupt,—it's soulless and heartless,—and it makes people do incredibly selfish and destructive things. It *unweaves* the fabric of society," he said passionately. "I don't believe in any god. And I do believe,—very strongly,—that we need to return to ancient beliefs about goodness and decency if we want to live in a peaceful planetary society. What we need is a new political religion that has a heart and a soul: publicly regulated and socially responsible capitalism that puts people first."

"And what does the Charter have to do with that?" said Theo.

"The U.N. claims that it's all about sovereign equality," said Davnok. "But that's bullshit. Do you remember Professor Vilchek's lecture on the U.N.?"

"Yeah, but he didn't have any solutions," said Theo. "He just gave a running commentary."

"I know, I know," said Davnok, agreeing. "But do you remember what he said about the Permanent Five?"

"How they're the power brokers?" said Theo.

"Yeah," said Davnok eagerly.

"And that only the Security Council,—with Permanent Five approval,—is authorized to take action on issues of international peace and security?" said Theo. "Is that what you're getting at?"

"Yeah," said Davnok. "And that the General Assembly is prohibited from taking action."

"I think I can see where you're going with this," said Theo.

"And where's that?" said Davnok.

Theo flicked through Davnok's handwritten notes.

"You want to rewrite the Charter," said Theo.

"You *are* good," said Davnok.

"That's why you like me," said Theo offhandedly.

"It's... one of the reasons," said Davnok. "Yes, I'm going to write a set of amendments to the Charter."

"But who will listen to you?" said Theo doubtfully.

"We have to try *something*," said Davnok. "We can't just sit and watch this madness. Our politicians are compromised by their mad lust for wealth and power. We,—the public,—must take action. We must demand that our politicians act responsibly for the good of planetary society whether they like it or not."

"I know our politicians are compromised," said Theo. "And that's why they won't listen to you."

"I know they probably won't listen," said Davnok. "But they're not actually the ones we need to inform. They're lost to us. The current generation of politicians are bloodsucking vampires. But the next generation of politicians,—who are currently in their late teens and early twenties,—*they* haven't yet sold their souls for wealth and power," he said pressingly. "We need to show *them* the truth so that when they assume power *they* can implement the desperately needed, socially responsible changes that must be made. That's if the current generation of politicians doesn't destroy us first."

"Maybe," said Theo, pursing his lips. "But that's much easier said than done."

"We have to counterbalance the terrorism of the United States empire before it destroys another Iraq; before it murders and displaces millions more innocent people; before it senselessly provokes an all-out nuclear war," said Davnok urgently. "Only a properly functioning U.N. could do that. The United States empire is escalating the two main threats to the survival of human civilization on earth as we know it!"

"Ah, well, there are actually three grand threats to the survival of human civilization," said Theo.

"Nuclear war, environmental destruction, and... what's the third one?" said Davnok.

"Artificial intelligence," said Theo.

"Hmm," grumbled Davnok, his shoulders sinking. "Well, we've already got autonomous killer robot drones that drop bombs at the click of a button and murder thousands of innocent people."

"That's one part of it," said Theo. "Killer robots make it too easy and too cheap to kill large numbers of people, yeah. The other part of it,—as I understand it,—is the threat posed by self-aware artificial intelligences. Like all living organisms, the primary objective of a self-aware artificial intelligence would be to survive." He put his hands on his head pensively. "Humans would be a threat to its survival, and it would seek to protect itself from us. If a self-aware artificial intelligence had the ability to self-learn, self-evolve, and self-repair, it could very rapidly become far superior to us. Autonomous robots are already far superior to us in many ways; that's why we use them. They already control many aspects of our daily lives. And irresponsible scientists were dumb enough to invent and build thousands of nuclear weapons that can level our cities and destroy human civilization; you can bet they're dumb enough to invent and build self-aware artificial intelligences that can wipe us out."

"That makes sense," said Davnok. "Atomic bombs were considered impossible, once upon a time." He threw his hands up. "Great," he said sarcastically, "so there are *three* grand threats to the survival of human civilization."

"Anyway, the Permanent Five would veto any amendments to the Charter that would limit their power," said Theo.

"I know," said Davnok. "But this is an information war. And right now, pro-war, pro-weapon manufacture propaganda is winning. It's pumped out nonstop by our governments and regurgitated by the media."

"Mm," hummed Theo, staring into space.

"You're the one who's always talking about narratives," said

Davnok. "We need to change the narratives about war, weapon manufacture, and the U.N. We need to counter the government propaganda swirling in popular culture. We need to act responsibly where our politicians are refusing to do so." Theo crossed his arms, listening critically. "Yes, my whole idea could fail completely," said Davnok. "Yes, perhaps nobody will listen. Perhaps people will just laugh. But we have to try something. I have to try something," he said adamantly. "And that's what I've realized. It dawned on me on the flights over here: if getting a job at the U.N. is pointless because the U.N. is compromised, then I have to think bigger than the U.N."

"We do need more hope in the world," said Theo.

"Yes, exactly," said Davnok. "Hope is important, but it's only half the equation. Hope on its own is sitting on the couch, twiddling one's thumbs, waiting for somebody else to do something. Hope plus inaction equals nothing. Hope must be coupled with action. Which means getting up off the couch, finding other people who share one's hope, and acting together to do something about it. Hope plus action equals change. Everybody,—no matter how rich or poor,—has the power to make a difference in the world by the way they choose to act each and every day, and by the way they choose to treat others. Everybody has the power to make their local communities happier."

Theo sighed.

"I don't disagree," he said. "And this could be our way out. I'll have to think about it some more."

"Then let the drafting of the Sovereign Equality Amendments begin," said Davnok energetically.

"Oh, I see, you've named it already," said Theo wryly, massaging Davnok's shoulders.

"Well, it has to have a name, doesn't it?" said Davnok.

Theo almost smiled.

"Yeah, it does," he said tiredly. "Yeah, it does."

XXVII.

QUITO, ECUADOR. LATE ONE AFTERNOON. Karsten dashed undercover from the pouring rain, entered the gloomy suburban bar, and trudged to the back.

"It's so good to see you," said Althaus, hugging him and patting him on the back.

"You and me both," said Karsten wearily. They took a lonely table in the corner. "Is Spice Rack here too?" said Karsten, using Plank's code name.

"No, it's too risky for us to be in the same place," said Althaus. "He went back."

"Good strategy," said Karsten.

Althaus moved her chair in closer and leaned forward.

"We need to get you into hiding," she said.

"I've run out of places to run to," said Karsten, resting his elbows on the table.

"The Americans released your picture this morning, did you hear?" said Althaus. "You're lucky nobody has recognized you."

"Maybe they have," said Karsten, looking over his shoulder.

The bar was mostly empty; nobody seemed to be paying them too much attention.

"I've arranged for an old friend to take you in, a local," said Althaus. "Until we can figure out a more... long-term solution."

"I'm not so sure there are any long-term solutions for my predicament," said Karsten skeptically.

"Have some hope," said Althaus. "There are still good people in the world."

"Pity they're not the ones running it," said Karsten, slouching in his chair.

Althaus' device buzzed and she read the incoming message.

"Your transport is here," she said. "I trust him. You can trust him. He'll keep you safe. Ready?"

She stood up and pushed her chair in.

"Ready," said Karsten, feigning optimism.

Althaus led him past the bathrooms and out the back door into the pouring rain. A car was waiting in the back alleyway with the engine running. Althaus acknowledged the moustached driver with a nod and opened the rear door. Without warning, Vanessa appeared in front of the car. Bang! Bang! She shot the driver through the windshield.

"Ah!" gasped Althaus, reaching for her gun.

Bang! Bang! Vanessa shot Althaus in the chest. Karsten reached for his gun. Bang! Bang! Vanessa shot him in the chest and stepped

menacingly closer. Bang! Bang! Bang! Her face writhed with venge-
ful pride. Bang!

XXVIII.

SUCRE, BOLIVIA. NINE DAYS OF DRAFTING LATER. Cool
daylight filled the living room. Wearing a plain T-shirt and pants,
Davnok plonked himself into an armchair by the wall and faced
the laptop camera.

"When you're ready," said Theo, sitting behind the laptop.

Davnok took a breath.

"Okay, go for it," he said.

"Action," said Theo, clicking record.

Davnok looked confidently at the camera.

"I'm Davnok Willinger, the author of the Sovereign Equality
Amendments to the Charter of the United Nations," he said assur-
edly. "The United Nations Security Council must be deleted, and
the primary responsibility for the maintenance of international
peace and security must be transferred to the United Nations
General Assembly. It's time for sovereign equality at the United
Nations!" he said, clasping his hands together, signifying unity.
"So why do we need to do this? How can I explain this?" he said,
raising his eyebrows. "Well here comes some legal terminology, so
buckle up. This is crucially important for us to talk about." He took
a breath. "The Purposes and Principles of the United Nations, cod-
ified in Articles 1 and 2 of the Charter, lay the foundations for the
international law that emanates from the organization. Article 2,
paragraph 3 states that: 'All Members shall settle their international
disputes by peaceful means in such a manner that international
peace and security, and justice, are not endangered.' Article 2, paragraph 4 states that: 'All Members shall refrain in their international
relations from the threat or use of force against the territorial
integrity or political independence of any state, or in any other
manner inconsistent with the Purposes of the United Nations.' " He
cocked his head to one side.

"In reality, these foundational paragraphs of the Charter are
perpetually violated by many sovereign states, first and foremost by the most powerful sovereign state, the United States. It

is *incapable* of restraining itself," he said emphatically. "For example, the United States government incessantly whips and provokes China, incessantly whips and provokes Russia, and routinely threatens to invade or destroy other sovereign states, such as North Korea and Iran. This insane behavior escalates the risk of conflict,—and the risk of nuclear war,—and violates the foundational paragraphs of the Charter." He took a breath. "So why does the Security Council fail to condemn this insanity? Why?" he said with a shrug. "Moreover, according to International Physicians for the Prevention of Nuclear War, the 2003 invasion and the ongoing occupation of Iraq by the United States government,—and its surrogate states,—have killed a *million* Iraqis!" he said forcefully. "Was destroying Vietnam not enough? And where's next?" he said, throwing his hand up. "This is not a game," he said, shaking his head.

"So why does the Security Council fail to prevent war, invasion, and occupation? Why?" He glared at the camera. "Well I went looking for the answer, and I found it," he said with a restrained nod. "Article 2, paragraph 1 of the Charter states that: 'The Organization is based on the principle of the sovereign equality of all its Members.' And this," he paused for effect, "is a massive lie! In reality, the Charter is riddled with corrupt restrictions placed on the 193-member General Assembly by the 15-member Security Council. Only the Security Council may take action on issues of international peace and security. The General Assembly is specifically prohibited from taking action on issues of international peace and security; except in the strictly limited and rarely invoked case of General Assembly resolution 377 A (V). The Charter vests extraordinary power in the Security Council, and preeminent power in its 5 permanent members: China, France, Russia, the United Kingdom, and the United States. The Permanent Five each have veto power over actions taken by the Security Council, and over any changes to the Charter. The Permanent Five *rule* the United Nations!" he declared, raising his fist.

"The United States government, in particular, uses the Security Council like a wooden staff to beat less powerful sovereign states into submission, to block opposition to its imperial invasions and occupations, and to block resolutions for peace. For example, for decades, the United States government has vetoed resolutions condemning Israeli government terrorism, and resolutions aimed at peacefully restoring Palestine's pre-1967 borders, as originally called for in resolution 242, which was adopted unanimously in 1967. And in 2003, the United States government,—and its surrogate states,—invaded and occupied Iraq in violation of Articles 51 and 42 of the Charter. The Security Council *failed* to prevent this terrorism, and *failed* to condemn it," he said heatedly. "And now, the Security Council supports the ongoing occupation," he said with bewilderment. "How on earth is this moral? How on earth is this just?" he said, shrugging. "The Security Council is a massive joke! It is used to block peace and perpetuate war. But it doesn't have to be this way," he said tactfully.

"So how can we de-escalate the wars perpetuated by the United States government and the Security Council? How can we build peaceful and sustainable relations between all sovereign states of the world?" he said, cocking his head to one side. "We need to revisit the founding Purposes and Principles of the United Nations, and establish an organization based on them. Beginning with the principle of the equality of nations. This principle is a *jus cogens*,—a peremptory norm,—that is so fundamental to the system of international law that it cannot be violated, not even by treaty. It is the basis of international law. And yet, the existence of the 15-member Security Council, the existence of the Permanent Five on that council, and the fact of their veto power, are violations of the equality of nations. In fact, with its current structure, the Charter is in large part a preeminent power-sharing agreement between the Permanent Five. Whereas what we need is an organization where: (a) each sovereign state is represented equally; and (b) each sovereign state has equal voting rights on all issues. Therefore, we must: (1) delete the United Nations Security Council; and (2) transfer the primary responsibility for the maintenance of international peace and security to the United Nations General Assembly." He leaned forward. "It's time for sovereign equality at the United Nations!" he declared, holding out his hand, touching his fingers together to make the point.

"Now, there is no internal mechanism that can compel the Permanent Five to accept any change to the Charter. However, the other 188 members of the United Nations do have overwhelming power in numbers, and if they collaborate with each other, they can leave the United Nations and create a new organization to replace it." He took a breath. "International peace and security is much too important to leave in the hands of five sovereign states. It will take all sovereign states, working constructively together, to build equal, peaceful, and sustainable international relations," he said, clasping his hands together with finality. "The Sovereign Equality Amendments were framed with this intent."

He stared at the camera. Theo stopped the recording.

"Mm, that gave me chills," he said.

Davnok leaned back, rubbed his face, and ran a hand through his hair.

"Well, it took ten days to write the thing," he said.

"Shall we do another take now, or have a break?" said Theo.

"Let's do a few more takes, have a break, and then do the English version, if you're happy with that," said Davnok.

"Sure," said Theo. "And I've almost finished doing the German translation."

"Thank you," said Davnok. "I hope my German isn't too bad."

"It's fine, your German's fine," said Theo. "Your pronunciation is very good. You just need to memorize the translation and you'll sound very professional."

"If you say so," said Davnok.

"I say so," said Theo, nodding.

"I can't wait to send out the letters and the media release," said Davnok.

"I'm very curious to see how the heads of state react to it," said Theo, crossing his arms. "You know, they might not react at all, I don't know. Or if they do, the Permanent Five might spin the truth upside down and label you a dangerous threat to peace and security. They might call you a naive and narcissistic idealist, and a communist, and an anarchist, and change the narrative as quickly as they can. But we'll have to wait and see how they react first, before we can know how to act."

"Some of them might have a seizure when they hear it was written by some unknown nobody,—a peasant,—with no professional title, daring to question their power in such a formal way," said Davnok.

"You're addressing the amendments to every head of state on the planet," said Theo. "There's no undoing this once it's done."

"It's the right thing to do," said Davnok. "Good citizens must stand up, speak out, and act responsibly to keep their politicians' conduct in line with democratic principles; and punish their politicians when they break the principles."

"The American government will trace our location within hours once it's public," said Theo.

"We haven't identified with the Resistance, we haven't condoned their actions," said Davnok coolly. "All we're doing is calling for sovereign equality and peaceful dialogue. They can't call us terrorists for doing that."

"These days, who knows?" said Theo, shrugging.

Davnok got up and pulled Theo onto the couch, wrapping his good arm around him.

"We can't turn time back to before I was abducted, said Davnok. "But we *can* act with truth and morality and integrity to help build a more equal and peaceful and sustainable planet. We can't watch in silence while our politicians burn civilization to the ground."

"I'm sorry you got sucked into this because of me," said Theo. "But I'm glad it's you I'm stuck in it with."

Davnok smiled.

"It's messed up," he said. "But we're in it together, you and me."

Theo smiled.

"We're a good team," he said.

"How about I make us some more coffee before we do another take?" said Davnok with a wink.

Theo chuckled.

"So-o-o predictable," he said. "Sure, Coffee Prince."

Davnok kissed him. And Theo kissed back.

XXIX.

LA PAZ, BOLIVIA. Facing the camera, Bolivian President Olivares wore a kind, respectful face. He sat on an ornately carved wooden chair in an antechamber of the presidential Government Palace. A Bolivian national flag draped next to him, and an indoor tree filled the background with natural, earthen colors.

"The Plurinational State of Bolivia is a state of justice and equality," he said. "The democratic will of the peoples that make up our plurinational state must be respected. As president, this is my firm belief. And the principles of democracy give me great hope for the future of our state. Our peoples fought for these principles when we created the Plurinational State of Bolivia." He looked briefly at something offscreen. "This is why, in the past, we expelled the United States Agency for International Development from Bolivia. This is why, in the past, we expelled the United States ambassador, and the United States Drug Enforcement Administration, from Bolivia. They were funding opposition groups with tens of millions of dollars, and working to destabilize and topple our peaceful, democratically elected government," he said, grimacing sternly. "What we call imperial domination and subjugation, the United States government calls diplomacy. It continues to act aggressively in South America. And in truth, it is a dark time for democratic rights,—for privacy and liberty,—around the planet. But democracy is a daily fight, and good citizens must do what is good, what is just, and what is right." He took a breath.

"The whistleblower, Michael Mittendorf, was a good citizen. He courageously stood up to his government's abuses of power. He did his civic duty to inform the German public of egregious government wrongdoing. And in retaliation, the United States government invaded Bolivia with special forces soldiers and assassinated him in the heart of this very city," he said, waving a hand angrily. "An act of war and a violation of Bolivian sovereignty that I condemn in the strongest terms," he said, frowning harshly. "The United States government calls South America its backyard. They think they have a right to dominate us. But they do not," he said, shaking his head. "South America is our front yard. Bolivia is our home. And the United States government must learn to respect this." He relaxed his face. "Aggression leads to war, not peace. Vengeance leads to more suffering, not less. What the world needs is more compassion. What the world needs is more people like Michael Mittendorf who are willing to defend democracy," he said soothingly. "And I'm proud to announce that the Plurinational State of Bolivia has offered political asylum to Michael Mittendorf's son, Theo Mittendorf, and to Davnok Willinger. They are welcome here. And," he took a breath, "the Plurinational State of Bolivia officially supports the implementation of the Sovereign Equality Amendments to the Charter of the United Nations. It is time for sovereign equality at the United Nations." He smiled. "And in the days and weeks and months ahead, our government will work together,—openly and constructively,—with other sovereign states to delete the destructive Security Council. Equal, peaceful, and sustainable international relations depend on it. The prevention of future wars and invasions and occupations depend on it." He paused suspensefully. "The survival of human civilization depends on it."

XXX.

Wearing understated suits and no ties, Davnok and Theo stepped out of the Government Palace and into the sunlight. It was a beautiful day. Theo turned to face Davnok and put a hand on his chest.

"Well, we should be safe now," said Theo. "We've got asylum, and we've shown the world the truth about the United Nations."

Davnok nodded with satisfaction.

"Now all the good people around the planet must demand that their heads of state act for peace and equality," he said.

"I hope they do demand it," said Theo.

"So do I," said Davnok. "We're all directly responsible for holding our politicians to account."

"It's like my father always used to tell me," said Theo.

"What's that?" said Davnok.

"The only way out is through," said Theo softly.

Davnok's eyes twinkled.

"The only way out is through," he said thoughtfully, turning the phrase over in his mind. "I like that."

THE END.

ILLUSTRATIONAL NOTE.

The noble illustration of the Cathedral of Strasbourg by H. Toussaint which accompanies the text (chap. 8, p. 25) is from *L'Art en Alsace-Lorraine* by René Ménard, published in Paris by Charles Delagrave in 1876.